RESCUE *at* FORT EDMONTON

Rita Feutl

RESCUE at FORT EDMONTON

Rita FEUTL

COTEAU BOOKS

WWW.COTEAUBOOKS.COM

Edited by Barbara Sapergia.
Cover painting by Dawn Pearcey.
Cover and book design by Duncan Campbell.
Typeset by Karen Steadman
Printed and bound in Canada by Transcontinental Printing.

Library and Archives Canada Cataloguing in Publication

Feutl, Rita, 1959-
Rescue at Fort Edmonton / Rita Feutl.

ISBN 1-55050-308-1

I. Title.

PS8611.E98R48 2004   jC813'.6   C2004-904619-5

10   9   8   7   6   5   4   3   2   1

Available in Canada & the US from:
Fitzhenry and Whiteside

401-2206 Dewdney Ave   195 Allstate Parkway
Regina, Saskatchewan   Markham, Ontario
Canada   S4R 1H3   Canada   L3R 4T8

The publisher gratefully acknowledges the financial assistance of the Saskatchewan Arts Board, the Canada Council for the Arts, the Government of Canada through the Book Publishing Industry Development Program (BPIDP), and the City of Regina Arts Commission, for its publishing program.

*To my father, Robert Feutl, whose kitchen-table tales
of empires and peasants and small, hungry boys
made history breathe for me.*

CHAPTER ONE

THE INSTANT SHE LAUNCHED HERSELF OVER THE CON-struction fence, one of those tiny warnings flashed through Janey Kane's mind.

The same uneasy feeling had nagged at her the time she was swimming off that beach in New Brunswick. The water had suddenly shifted from cool to cold, and a sense of something not quite right made Janey turn back to shore. Later that evening, her dad had talked about the dangerous undercurrents when the tide was turning.

And there was the time even earlier, when Janey had leapt from the top of the basement stairs. It was only after she'd launched herself from the landing that something told her she'd jumped from too high up. Though she'd tried flapping her arms frantically to stop herself from falling, there was no going back. Janey came out of that escapade with a cast on her arm and a new respect for heights.

But here, at this construction pit inside historical Fort Edmonton Park, height really wasn't a problem. There was just a silly fence surrounding the building site, and a lot of mud on the other side where they were digging the foundation for some sort of old-fashioned airport hangar. Still, Janey regretted her leap the instant her feet left the ground. One second she was casually swinging the locket in the bright sunshine, and the next she was following its arc over the fence and into the pit where it lay in all that mud. Her new white sneakers were going to be toast.

But when Janey's feet touched the ground, her running shoes were the least of her worries. Instead of coming to a messy, mucky landing, Janey just kept going, plummeting through the topsoil and *into* the earth. Thrashing frantically, she tried to find solid footing. First she was in up to her knees, then her waist. Too horrified to shout or call out, Janey realized she was being pulled into, and under, the collapsing ground, even as she reached desperately for handfuls of crumbling earth.

Kicking and grabbing at anything that could give her support, Janey fought the fear that was building inside her as quickly as the ground was sucking her in. She wanted to shout, call out, cry for help, but it was too late. She'd slipped underground, with soil pressing in on every last bit of her – hair, ears, nose, mouth – and she could feel herself sliding further and further away from sunlight and warmth. Eyes squeezed tightly shut, Janey pulled one arm over her mouth to keep the dirt from going in as she plummeted toward what surely had to be the centre of the earth.

Suddenly the sliding stopped. It took a moment to realize she was still breathing. It took another moment to realize that the thunderous pounding she heard was not from anything outside, but from her heart, which was beating louder than she'd ever heard it. With her other arm pinned under her and still unable to open her eyes, Janey tried to move. Nothing hurt, and even better, she could shift her legs. Struggling, she pulled her knees to a crouching position and yanked her upper body out of the dirt. She opened her eyes.

The air was heavy and humid and deeply, liquidly black. It was so dark that Janey brought her hands to her face to make sure that her eyes were really open. They were, but she couldn't see the fingertips in front of her, let alone the space she was in. Carefully, she reached out to touch her surroundings. Earth all around her, but hard-packed, except for where she'd just landed. Could she dig her way through to the outside? She scrambled over the loose dirt, clawing at it furiously, only to realize that the more she dug, the more it crumbled down from overhead.

Slumping down beside the pile of dirt she'd created, Janey felt a second wave of panic. Here she was, alone, buried in some pit in a city half a continent away from her home, and nobody knew where she was.

She'd always known it was a bad idea for her parents to send her out to Edmonton.

THE TWO-YEAR-OLD IN THE LAST ROW squealed as the airplane's altitude dropped suddenly, then levelled out. The fasten-your-seat belt light pinged on overhead, and the pilot's voice crackled over the airplane's loudspeaker.

"Just an air pocket, folks," he said reassuringly. "But we're approaching Edmonton in a few minutes, so you may as well leave your seat belts on and prepare for landing."

Janey had refused to look up from her book when the plane made that stomach-dropping dip, even though she'd noticed, from the corner of her eye, how the woman beside her had gripped the armrest until her knuckles were white. Serves her right, thought Janey; she should have let me have some elbow room on the armrest during the flight.

Even when the flight attendants came down the aisle to collect headphones and blankets, Janey refused to look up. Luckily she'd turned twelve this spring, and didn't have to fly as an Unaccompanied Minor with those dorky plastic pouches around her neck. And she didn't have to put up with the attendants' cheery smiles and fake friendly voices. The last thing she needed was someone nattering on about how excited she must be to see her grandmother after all these years.

Why would she be excited? Who'd be thrilled about leaving *all* her friends – friends she'd worked hard to make when her family had moved to that new Toronto neighbourhood three years ago – to go halfway across the country to Edmonton, of all places? Who'd ever heard of Edmonton? Who'd *want* to go to there, when you could spend the sweetest summer possible in Canada's biggest city? And this was such an important summer, what with finishing elementary school and finally heading off to junior high, and planning for that first day back with Becca and Kira and

Rachel. But now she was here, heading off into the boon-docks, torn from her best friends and everything she'd ever known and loved. She'd bet Granny didn't even have a computer; how was she supposed to talk to her friends?

Fuming, Janey finally glanced out the window. Oh, man, she groaned inwardly, just look at this place. One field after another down there, all patched together like a giant quilt. In fact, it was *just* fields down there. Where were the people? Who lived out here except old folks and maybe some cowboys? She couldn't even see any stupid cows. She bet the cowboys were just for show anyway. Man, this summer was just going to be the biggest disaster *ever*.

If it hadn't been for her mum getting that dumb job in Turkey for the season, life would have been perfect. But no. Her mum had to go and apply to help after they'd had some stupid earthquake over there.

"You're not being fair!" Janey had hollered after her mother explained that she'd been asked to help design new housing for survivors. "Why can't you do that stuff here in your office at home, the same as always?"

"Janey, it's a wonderful opportunity for me," said her mum patiently. "It's taken years to put together my ideas, and I need to be there to watch it develop."

"Well, then, why can't I just stay here with Daddy? At least he's not going anywhere."

"Honey, you know your father has to work very hard and often doesn't come home until late. And he's got a couple of business trips out to Seattle this summer that he just can't put off. In fact, he's hoping to make stopovers so he can see you for a few days while you're in Edmonton."

"I don't want to see him for a few days," Janey wailed. "I want you and Daddy to be around for the whole summer. Here. At home. With me."

Janey's mum looked pained. "Sweetie," she said, trying to draw Janey into her arms.

"No!" Janey cried, breaking away from her mum's grasp. "All you want to do is what YOU want and you don't even care about what *I* want. I don't want to go and I'm not going."

Not even the resounding thwack of her bedroom door slamming made her feel any better.

But here she was, three weeks later, about to land in a place she'd never been, with no friends, for the entire summer. She hardly even knew her grandmother, who'd flown out to Toronto four years ago for the Christmas holidays. All she'd remembered was her mother muttering about the filthy ashtrays all over the house. In desperation, Janey'd tried to use her grandmother's smoking as a reason not to go.

"Granny Kane says she's quit smoking, Janey," her mum had said, when confronted as she worked at the computer. "And I have enough faith in you about smoking to know that you and Granny won't be sucking cigarettes on the front stoop every evening." She had clicked her mouse and the printer had begun spitting out blueprints.

"But what about *my* health if she still smokes around me?" Janey had grumped over the printer's whine. "All that second-hand smoke; and my pores and my tender young lungs...and they don't really sit on the front stoop every night out there, do they?"

"Honey, Granny's quit. As for the front stoop, no, I don't think they do that anymore, though according to your father, his childhood was straight out of a 1950s TV show." Janey's mum had closed the file on her screen and turned to her daughter.

"Janey, it won't be that bad. There's an outdoor pool about a block away; there's that huge mall with all the fun stuff in it, and it might be nice to spend a little time with Granny. Remember when Daddy flew out to spend a week with her in the spring? She was after him then to let you come out for the summer. She's been on her own since Grampa died all those years ago and I think she could really use the company."

Sure, thought Janey, grimly stuffing her book into her backpack as the airplane descended. Granny'd need something to break up the monotony of life on the front stoop, swinging away in her rocking chair, watching the cows clatter on home.

JANEY FIGURED SHE WAS GOING TO ACT COOL and haughty when she greeted her grandmother at the arrivals gate. But when she couldn't see anyone with grey hair who looked like the photos at home, she headed for her luggage. A hand on her arm stopped her. Janey turned to see a blonde woman holding out her arms.

"Hello, kiddo," said her gravel-voiced grandmother. "What? You can't remember what I look like?"

"Granny, your hair..." Janey said, allowing herself to be

folded into her grandmother's hug. The wiry arms wrapped themselves around her and Janey felt herself being squeezed until she could hardly breathe.

"Oh, yeah, I forgot you guys haven't seen me since I decided to go blonde," said Granny, releasing Janey and stepping back. "Whaddya think? I just figured I needed to shake up my life a little; do something new for myself."

Janey eyed her grandmother critically. Same loose, long body, same shrewd eyes watching her, same jeans-and-T-shirt kind of Granny as the one in the photos. Maybe a little skinnier, the hair definitely blonder, and the glasses were almost funky – the type Becca craved if she could only get an eye doctor to give her a prescription. Becca constantly bemoaned the fact that she was cursed with 20/20 vision.

"Not bad," said Janey, recognizing that she was being inspected as well, and that her grandmother was drinking in Janey's hazel eyes, shoulder-length brown hair and new height. Much to Janey's embarrassment, she'd shot up over the last year, and now towered over all her friends, never mind the boys in her class. She was glad Granny didn't say anything about her height. For a second Janey wondered if her grandmother had also been a tall, gawky twelve-year-old.

Granny looped her arm through Janey's and swept her granddaughter toward the luggage carousel, where suitcases were already lumbering around the track.

"Let's get your gear and head on home. I've left chili cooking on the stove and it needs a stirring."

Janey's second surprise was Granny's car. Long and old and glinting with chrome, it glowed bright yellow from the corner of the lot where Granny had carefully parked it.

"Yup, that's my Cadillac," said Granny proudly. "I call her Marilyn, on account of the colour."

"Cool car," said Janey. "Did you just buy it?"

"Nope. She belonged to your grampa. She sat in a barn for years up in Morinville. Two years after Grampa died, I got a call from the farmer asking if I still wanted to pay for her storage. I drove up and rescued her, and about five years ago I decided she needed a colour job. Mine came later," said Granny, patting her hair. "We've both been around the block a few times, but we're holding together pretty well. Hop in."

They raced into the city, past fields and tractors and – yes – large herds of cows. Great, thought Janey, we *will* be watching them amble down our street. But she could see a skyline in the distance, and when they finally turned onto busy Whyte Avenue, it looked enough like a real city that Janey figured they might be safe from wandering livestock.

Granny's house was tiny, a two-bedroom wartime bungalow with an apartment in the basement – Granny called it a suite – that she rented out every fall to university students. "It helps cover the bills," she explained, "and besides, I like the company."

Janey's room was in the back of the house, overlooking a large garden divided neatly into grassy areas and plots of dug-up earth. "I haven't been able to get out as much this spring," said Granny, coming to stand beside her grand-daughter at the window. "I was hoping maybe you could give me a hand."

As if, thought Janey, recalling the tiny, pocket-sized yard at the back of her Toronto house. Their landlord had paved half of it, and the other side took about a pack and a half of flower seeds to keep her dad happy. Janey wasn't planning on getting her hands dirty this summer. She turned back toward the room without saying anything. That's when she saw the locket.

It was lying on the pillow of what was to be her bed, the silver glinting in the late afternoon sun.

"I thought you might like a welcome gift," said Granny, as Janey moved toward the quilt-covered bed. "It belonged to my mother and I felt it was time you should have it."

"Cool," said Janey, studying the thin oval pendant, delicately engraved with intertwined leaves. She fumbled with the clasp.

"There's a photograph of me as a baby in there, and one of your great-grandfather, just before he died of diphtheria. My mother loved that locket. She always wore it."

Janey stared at the black-and-white photos of a solemn young toddler in ringlets, ribbons, and a frilly gown and an equally serious man with a pointy beard and high, starched collar.

"If you don't like the pictures, you can always put your own in."

"They're kinda cool, Granny. They look so old-fashioned. Can I wear the locket?"

"Of course you can. That's what it's for. I put a new chain on it so it would be nice and strong. I'm glad you like it."

Granny turned away, stopped, then turned back. "If

you're interested in old stories, I thought tomorrow we might go to the historical park we have here in Edmonton. It's not flashy and full of zippy rides, but it's got some nice old buildings and a reconstructed Hudson's Bay Company trading fort that might tell you a little bit about where you've come from. Stuff about early settlers, and First Nations people."

"You mean it's all about history?" Janey's heart sank.

"Yeah, but the way they do it is sort of interesting. The people working there dress up in the clothes from that time. They've even got whole families who volunteer there, with kids all done up in bonnets and breeches..."

Great. History and Halloween all rolled into one. That's all she needed, thought Janey. But as she glanced at the locket in her hand, she figured she ought to do something nice in return for Granny's gift. One day wouldn't kill her.

WELL, IT NEARLY HAS, THOUGHT JANEY, trapped in the dark in what seemed like the centre of the earth. She'd gone to the stupid park, and watched her grandmother ooh and ah over old washboards and young men dressed in bowler hats and vests. Most of the interpreters, which is what the costumed people called themselves, were university students, but some, as her grandmother had said, were volunteers, from toddlers to seniors, all decked out in old-fashioned clothes.

None of it really grabbed Janey's attention. While her grandmother was poking through some dumb farmhouse, Janey'd wandered over to the horses. Bored, she'd taken off her new necklace, and whipped the chain around on her finger. The locket swung around like a demented one-bladed helicopter propeller.

When the horses realized she had nothing to feed them, they ambled back to the barn. Janey wandered over to the other side of the corral, crossing the rails of the old steam engine that thundered past every half-hour or so.

On the other side of the tracks was a huge, chewed-up field, surrounded by fencing. "Future home of the Blatchford Field Hangar," read the sign at the front. Janey wandered over to look at the work-in-progress, swinging her locket. When it flew over, she just seemed to fly in after it.

And now here she was, trapped underground in some creepy pit. And after all that, she didn't even have the locket with her. What was Granny going to say? Janey'd barely had the thing for twenty-four hours and she'd already lost it. How could she have been so careless with such an old piece of jewellery?

Jewellery! That was it! She still had her watch on, the one with the light-up face. Quickly, Janey pushed the small button on the side, and an eerie green glow lit up the space. She undid the watch strap and used the tiny light to explore her surroundings. She was in a cave, she realized, and as she moved the watch around, she discovered four tunnels leading away from the collapsed roof. Now what?

She released her watch light. Peering into each tunnel in turn, Janey thought she detected a glimmer of light at the end of the one with the smallest opening. She thrust her little light into it, where it glimmered weakly in the dark.

What if she ran into some kind of awful animal? What did they have out here anyway? Did skunks live underground? Porcupines? What did you do if you met one?

But there was no sense just sitting still. She strapped her watch back on. "Here goes," she muttered aloud, and wedged herself into the opening. Hardly big enough to crawl in, the tunnel forced Janey to wriggle past rocks and stones that scratched her bare arms and legs. But the light was growing bigger and brighter, and Janey sensed she was moving uphill toward outside air.

At last she reached the opening. Pulling herself from the hole, Janey tried to stand, but her knees gave way. She collapsed onto the grass and glanced around. No airport hangar construction here. No horses, no barn, no old farmhouse with Granny inside. She must have crawled a good distance underground to some other part of the park.

She was in a field surrounded by scrubby bush. At one end, a pond glinted in the sunshine. Janey watched as a deer wandered daintily forward and lowered its head for a drink.

They keep deer in this park? Cool, thought Janey, and then realized that she, too, was thirsty. She stood up again, this time more steadily, and glanced down at herself. "Oh man, just look at me!" she wailed, sending the deer skittering. Her new GAP T-shirt, the one she'd wheedled her mum into buying, was streaked with muck, as were the pink shorts she'd matched it with. Determinedly, she headed toward the pond. If she washed it off right away, it wouldn't stain as badly.

With the deer gone, Janey had the pond all to herself.

She waded in up to her knees, realized how warm it was, and impulsively took a shallow dive into the water.

It felt good to get the mud out of her hair. She could even feel it loosening from her eyelashes. Coming to the surface, she flipped over onto her back, and did a lazy crawl to the other side of the pond. This isn't so bad, she thought, the water swirling while the sun warmed her face. She floated languidly, relishing the light that penetrated her closed eyelids after the darkness of the tunnels. She wondered what Rachel and Kira were up to.

A splash quite close to her snapped her out of her reverie. Pulling her feet beneath her, Janey trod water and searched the shoreline. Two rocks flew toward her, and then the pond was peppered with them. Someone was using her for target practice and getting close to the mark. Janey swam the other way, but saw, from the corner of her eye, two boys – no, three of them, in dirty shirts and odd-looking shorts that seemed to gather below the knee – running around the edge of the pond, flinging stones as they went.

"Hey, stop that, you idiots! This is not funny!" Janey shouted, veering away from their aim.

"Ha! Ha! Look at her. Betcha she's got no clothes on! Let's get her!" shouted the biggest, nastiest looking one of the bunch.

What jerks! More angry than frightened, Janey swam backwards. "Stop it!" she called sharply. Jeering, the boys ignored her, firing their ammunition ever faster. One rock caught her arm, then another nicked her side as it sank under the water. This was getting serious. Should she head back to the centre of the pond? But she'd be a sitting duck for them there. Instead, she turned and swam toward the opposite beach. Her knees scraped the muck at the bottom and she struggled to stand. But another rock caught her on her shoulder blade, and she threw herself forward onto the beach.

Abruptly, the shouting stopped. Janey raised her head slightly, and came nose to toes with a pair of beautifully embroidered moccasins. There were feet in the moccasins, she realized. Janey's eyes rose higher, past a pair of trousers and a long-sleeved shirt and an oddly formal vest, until they came to the face of a tall, dark-eyed man with black braids hanging past his shoulders.

"Can you help me?" she asked. The man nodded, turned and walked into the bush. "Hey, wait a minute!" Janey called out, annoyance and fright mixed equally in her voice. She knew that the boys, though quiet, were still somewhere around the pond. Heaving herself out of the water, she stumbled toward the bushes where she'd last seen her rescuer.

CHAPTER TWO

"HEY! WAIT UP!" JANEY SHOUTED, PANTING AND stumbling through the underbrush. She may as well have been talking to the poplars and pine trees surrounding her; the man up ahead didn't stop. Her waterlogged running shoes squelched a muddy staccato as she dodged branches and tree roots.

What kind of a stupid park was this? she wondered. Sinkholes in construction sites, killer kids around the pond, and now this guy pretending to be a Native Indian, who couldn't even show her how to get out of here.

"Hey! You! Just because you've got a role to play in this dumb park doesn't mean you can't talk to me normally. Can't you wait up and tell me how to get out of here?" she called.

It was no use. Her guide slipped through the trees and Janey crashed along behind. Just when she figured she'd take her chances with the three idiots by the pond, they reached a clearing in the brush.

"Oh, man – I *knew* I'd run into cows while I was here," Janey wailed. And not just one or two. Grazing contentedly in the pasture ahead of her were dozens and dozens of caramel-coloured beasts, placidly chewing away while Janey stared at them in horror.

"Mister! What if those cows attack me! I have an uncle who's a lawyer! We'll...we'll sue you. We'll take this park to the cleaners!" she called. No answer. Weaving his way calmly through the cows, the man was making for an odd, round structure at the far end of the field. Janey skittered after him, stepping in two cow pies as she tried to keep up.

The man reached the curiously shaped building and slipped around it. Following him, Janey caught a whiff of hay, animals, and something earthier. Of course! It was a barn, and there, across the field, was a farmhouse, which her guide had already reached.

The white of the apron on the woman who opened the screen door was the first thing Janey noticed. There was so much of it, starting near the grey-haired woman's chin and dropping down to just above her ankles. Not that Janey saw any ankles. A dark skirt peeked out underneath the apron, but the woman's long-sleeved blouse was rolled up to the elbows. She must be boiling in that getup, thought Janey. These park people took their jobs way too seriously.

"Good day, Omâcîw," said the woman. "Is your wife still feeling poorly?"

The man spoke in a language that made absolutely no sense to Janey.

"Now wait a minute," fumed Janey as she approached the door. "This is taking this whole reality thing a bit too far."

As the Native man continued to speak, the woman's eyes swept over Janey. "The Jameson boys caught you swimming at the pond, did they?" she said when he'd finished. "Well, you're not likely to see your clothes again – they're probably buried behind their outhouse by now."

She turned back to the man. "Thank you, Omâcîw. Before you go, please take along some of my spruce and tansy tea for your wife. It's the least I can do after her mother showed me what it was good for."

She stepped inside and returned with a fragrant bundle wrapped in white cloth. Omâcîw took the bundle and turned to retrace his steps. The woman beckoned Janey. "Step inside and I'll see if I can come up with some of Mag's old things – she's my youngest, but a bit older than you, I'd imagine," she said. "By the way, I'm Mrs. Henderson. You must not be from around here. I can't say as I recognize your face."

"Oh, I'm Janey Kane. I'm from Toronto, but I'm visiting my grandmother in Edmonton for the summer, and we came out here to look around and then I fell into this hole and crawled through the mud and then those stupid boys pelted me with rocks..."

"Child, I can't stand here all day letting flies into the house," said Mrs. Henderson firmly. "I'll find you some things and then you can ride into Edmonton with Anna. She's promised to stop by and take a case of my butter to the market." She was about to turn away when she glanced at

Janey's T-shirt. "I can't say I've heard of the GAP milling company. Peculiar name. Must be some kind of new Eastern flour. Out here we make our underwear from Brackman & Kerr flour sacks. Wipe those feet on the scraper before you come in."

Puzzled, Janey did as she was told, then entered a good-sized kitchen. A tangy, unfamiliar scent mixed with the pungent smell of herbs drying over the stove. Bowls and buckets covered with cloth crowded the table. A water pump crouched over a sink in one corner, while in another corner stairs rose to the second floor.

"I'll see what I can find," said Mrs. Henderson as she disappeared up the stairs. "You may sit down by the table. Mind you don't upset the buttermilk."

Janey lifted the tea towel that covered the bowl closest to her and the tangy scent grew stronger. That white, thick-looking stuff must be the buttermilk, she thought. She let the cloth drop and wandered over to the cast-iron stove across from the sink. It radiated heat. How on earth could you cook over a fire on a hot day like today? she wondered.

Arms full of clothes, Mrs. Henderson returned to the room and thrust them at Janey.

"Here. I know the style's a bit old-fashioned to someone from Toronto, but these will make you presentable until you can meet up with your grandmother. And if I can't find Mag's old straw hat, the sunbonnet I use in the garden will do."

Janey nearly burst out laughing as she inspected the bundle

of clothes. Long – really, *really* long – black, scratchy-looking socks topped the pile. Not a chance, she thought. Underneath, she discovered a soft white petticoat and a long, navy blue cotton dress that appeared to button up the back. Last in the pile was a huge white cotton apron.

"Best get on with it," continued Mrs. Henderson. "Anna will be here presently and I don't want the butter to stand out in the heat." She stood, hands on hips, waiting for Janey to dress. "I'll help you with the buttons on the back. Then you may have a glass of buttermilk before you set out."

"But I don't want to wear all this stuff," said Janey, eyeing the layers with dismay.

"Well, you can't go prancing around town in your under-drawers, child! The very idea!" She bustled over, popped the petticoat over Janey's head and drew her arms into the sleeves.

"But this is on top of what I'm already wearing!" Janey wailed. Physically resisting this commanding woman seemed, somehow, impossible.

"Oh, for goodness sake! Don't tell me they're wearing their camisoles *over* their petticoats in Toronto! What a queer idea. Here, let's get this dress on you; I can hear Anna's wagon coming up the hill."

"But, but –" Janey's sputtering protest was muffled as Mrs. Henderson yanked the dress on top of her. She spun the bewildered girl around, buttoned up the back, tied the apron over top, and plonked a straw hat on her head.

"I'm assuming you can put the stockings on yourself. I need to get the butter." Mrs. Henderson swept out of the kitchen, leaving the screen door shuddering in her wake.

Janey had never been so hot in her life. But she couldn't reach the buttons behind her, and it was almost too hot to try. Instead, she rolled the long woollen socks into a ball and looked for a place to hide them. She opened a door on a tall cupboard beside her, but a great hunk of dripping ice blocked her way. Inside the next door was better – the metal-lined container held shelves filled with pitchers of milk and blocks of butter. She thrust her hand behind two jugs and dropped the socks, then closed the door reluctantly on the cool interior just as Mrs. Henderson returned.

She was followed by a dark-haired, black-eyed girl who stared curiously at Janey. "Anna Hirczi, this is Janey Kane," said the older woman. Groggy, hot and uncomfortable, Janey stared miserably at the slim girl who was dressed much like her, but moved with a cool, fluid grace to accept a glass of buttermilk from Mrs. Henderson.

Janey took hers with more suspicion. Tiny beads of condensation gathered on the rim of Janey's glass as she considered when she'd last had buttermilk. Probably never. But Anna had already emptied her own glass and was still eyeing her inquisitively.

Here goes nothing, Janey thought, and took a small sip. Cool and slightly sour, it tickled the back of her throat as it went down. The next sip went down more smoothly, and in half a second, her glass was empty. "Refreshing on a hot day, isn't it?" asked Mrs. Henderson. Surprised, Janey nodded, and wondered briefly if buttermilk Slurpees would ever make it at the corner store.

"Off you go," said Mrs. Henderson, holding the screen

door open. Anna was already in the wagon. "Once you find your grandmother, Janey, you can send the clothes back with Anna."

With pleasure, thought Janey, hot and clammy once more as she climbed up into the wagon.

IT WASN'T UNTIL THEY DESCENDED the hill and rounded the corner that anyone spoke. Janey could tell Anna'd been watching her, but when they lost sight of the house, Janey turned to her and said: "Look, you may want to go on playing this game, but I can't stand it anymore. You've got to help me out of these clothes. Aren't you roasting?"

Anna stared at her. "Mrs. Henderson said you are a small bit strange. What is wrong with these clothes? With the new styles the skirts are now shorter, but if you are older, then long is still good. How old are you?"

"I'm twelve, and I'm boiling. Look, stop this wagon. Are all of you guys weird? Man, I can't wait to get out of this stupid place." Janey jerked around to try to catch a button on her apron, and accidentally popped one off.

Anna caught the button before it rattled off the wagon seat. "Here. I will help you with the pinny, even though it makes your dress more cheerful," she said, undoing the row of tiny white fasteners.

"Don't stop. Do the dress too," urged Janey after the apron came loose. "I can't reach the dress buttons."

"What? You cannot waltz into the city in your petticoat," said Anna.

"I've got shorts on underneath!" Janey shrieked, exasperated. "Look!"

"But...you are not wearing any stockings," said Anna, awed, looking at Janey's bare legs. "And such shoes! What are these? A Toronto moccasin?"

"Oh, quit fooling around. Those are my sneakers, for Pete's sake. We all wear this in Toronto," said Janey impatiently, squirming until she could reach the buttons on the back of her dress. "Why didn't they design dresses back then so a girl could get them on and off without any help?" Furious, she lifted the dress and the petticoat over her head and flung them into the back of the wagon. "What time period is this supposed to be anyway?"

Anna's eyes just about bugged out of her head. She brought the pony to a stop, then looked at Janey with a mixture of fear and pity. "Now look," she said soothingly, "we will find your grandmamma and she will take care of you, but to walk through the streets with only these clothes is...not right! No good! What is the matter with you? Even in Toronto at the train station last year the ladies did not show such legs. Now in 1907 they change this much? No. You must put on the dress," said Anna firmly.

Janey had just about had it. "Would you stop playing around," she demanded furiously, stamping her foot and startling the pony. "It's not 1907 – give me a break! I am sick and tired of being in these stupid olden days. Look. Forget about my grandmother. Just take me to entrance of the park. Man, are they going to get an earful from me. What a stupid place. And you – how can you even be working today when it's sweltering like this? You must be crazy; the whole lot of you."

"Just look who is crazy," said Anna, reaching her own boiling point. "You scare poor Rosa, you take all your clothes off, you talk about a park...what park? Did those Jameson boys hit you on the head? You are either crazy or...rude."

"I am usually not either," said Janey through gritted teeth. "But you seem to be both."

Anna pulled the pony up short. "I do not want you here beside me any more. I like Mrs. Henderson, but you are just making me trouble. Go. Get out!"

When Janey didn't move, Anna pulled out the switch fastened to the side of her cart. "All right, all right," said Janey grumpily, putting her hands up in mock surrender. "I'm sorry I said you were crazy or...or rude. Look. I'm lost. I'll sit here and be quiet and good until we get to somewhere familiar."

"Then put at least the dress back on," said Anna, pushing her advantage. Janey sighed, and tugged the dress toward her. "And put this button away. You must sew it back before you can return the pinny."

Janey shoved the button into a pocket in her shorts, and put the navy dress back on. This was just the weirdest, craziest place she'd ever visited. She sighed and glanced at her watch. It still showed the same time she'd seen in the tunnel, which meant her watch had stopped working. She must have damaged it in the fall.

"A very fine watch you have," said Anna, obviously trying to be friendly.

"Thanks. But it doesn't seem to be working. What time is it anyway?"

"It is before noon," said Anna, "because I am hungry. We will eat when we get back."

Noon? It was past three when she jumped into that construction pit. All these people were just too weird for words. Her friends would never believe this. Nothing like this had ever happened to her in Toronto. The girl beside her was so into her role that it was a bit scary. She even spoke with an accent; did they teach you this stuff before you started working here? How old was she?

"Same like you – almost. In July I am twelve," Anna said, when Janey asked.

"Aren't you a little young to be working at a job?"

"Oh, this is not working. We need the bottles in the back, and Mrs. Henderson, she will give us some butter to pay. But this is no job. My brother Peter, he has a job with Papa in the coal mines. Peter is very proud – only ten years and already wages, but Mama and I, we do not like. Nobody like the mining now."

"Only ten years old?" Janey asked, caught up in this story despite herself.

"Yes, ten years, but as big as me," said Anna, smiling proudly. Then her face sobered. "We had also a little sister, Liesl, just four. But she died – a fever, very bad – in the Old Country. I think that is why we come here. Much land, no bad memories."

This girl was really playing her part, thought Janey, looking at Anna's sad face. She prodded her companion. "So what's wrong with the mining? I guess it's kinda dirty."

Anna snorted. "Pah. Dirt shows you work. Dirt is good. No. It is the fire. Do you remember?" She paused. "Ach, yes. You are from Toronto. When did you come? Yesterday? Then you did not see the fire, or hear it… It was terrible…" Anna kept her eyes on the placid Rosa's rump, but in her mind she was seeing something else.

"Tell me," Janey prodded.

"It was very late – all of us sleeping," Anna began. "Suddenly the bells from the churches, they were ringing and ringing. We came out from our tents and we could see, across the river, a big fire, and the sky was bright like the middle of the day. At first, it looked, somehow, beautiful.

"But right away the men knew it was a coal mine fire. Then we were all afraid, because there are so many mines and we did not know which one. And then we heard it was John Walter's mine and four men were trapped inside.

"From across the river we heard wives and mothers crying, screaming." She shook her head and looked directly at Janey. "Papa's friend, Mr. Lamb, he tried to go down to rescue them, but they could not climb back up the ladder. Mr. Lamb, he climbed out again, but the fire, it burned him very bad."

Her voice dropped almost to a whisper. "Papa says he screamed all night before he died."

The wagon paused while a goat and several chickens meandered across the path. Anna urged Rosa forward again and continued. "Mr. Lamb's sister will receive a medal from the English king because her brother was so brave, but

Mama says if the owners made the mines more safe, he did not need to be brave. Now, we worry every time Papa and Peter go to work. And sometimes, the wind, when it blows, I think I still hear Mr. Lamb – his screams..."

Severely spooky, thought Janey, as Anna lapsed into silence. They were nearing the river's edge; the trees and bushes fell away and they passed small shanties and ramshackle lean-tos. Chickens pecked in the dirt and the occasional dog warned them about coming too close to a shed. Woodsmoke scented the air. Rosa plodded steadily toward a bridge in the distance. Janey was nearly lulled to sleep.

But when she glanced across the river and up the opposite embankment, a sudden shiver stole up Janey's neck. "Anna, is this Edmonton ahead?"

When the other girl nodded, goosebumps joined Janey's shivers. The impressive skyline of tall, modern buildings built with concrete and chrome that had consoled her yesterday on her drive into the city had disappeared. Instead, a few rickety wooden buildings clung to the top of the embankment, while the slopes leading to the river teemed with horses, pedestrians, and ramshackle housing of every sort.

Where were the paved roads, the traffic lights, the cars and trucks she'd seen yesterday? Prickles crept up her sides and her hands grew clammy. Janey panicked. What's going on here? she wondered. Maybe those boys did hit my head. Or maybe I was hurt in the tunnel, without realizing it.

"I fell into that hole..." said Janey, almost to herself.

"What's that?" asked Anna.

"I said, I fell into that hole, and it was terribly dark and maybe I'm really still there. Maybe I'm just dreaming all this. What year did you say this was?"

Anna snorted and pinched Janey on her leg. "Ow!" shrieked Janey. "What'd you do that for?"

"When you dream, a pinch does not hurt so much," said Anna smugly. "You are here, and Edmonton is before you and the time is 1907."

Slowly, with a creeping sense of dreadful certainty, Janey came to a horrible realization – against all the laws of physics, Anna was right. Somehow Janey had travelled almost one hundred years into the past.

What was she doing here? How was she going to get back? The cart had made it down to the bridge and Rosa was clopping steadily across. Maybe Janey should jump out, go back? But she didn't want to face those awful boys again, and how was she supposed to find that tunnel? Hadn't Anna said the area was riddled with mines?

Desperately, she cast her eyes over the embankment ahead. She was shocked to discover that many of the buildings were tents, made from dirty canvas in various shapes and sizes. Many were fronted by garden plots, and a few had goats and even cows tethered to a corner of the tent. Women sewed or cooked at small firepits while children with balls and hoops dodged the pegs and tethered animals.

"Anna...these people...they live here? In these tents?"

Anna giggled. "Yes. We also live in a tent. Papa says there are thousands of us here in Edmonton, making camp like cowboys."

"But why don't you just get a house? How long have you lived like this?"

"Since we came in the fall we are living in a tent. Building supplies cost great money and are hard to find."

"But all winter?"

"Oh, yes, but Papa and Peter, they put straw bales all around the walls and we are warm like – how do you say? – bugs." She grinned triumphantly at Janey, then pulled Rosa to a stop. "Here we are."

A woman with a brightly coloured kerchief over her head appeared from behind a large canvas structure. *"Gut gegangen, Anna?"* she asked before her eyes landed on Janey.

"Mama, this is Janey Kane. She was at Mrs. Henderson's and she is coming with me to the market."

Mrs. Hirczi held out her hand and smiled. "You are welcome," she said.

"Thank you," said Janey, awkwardly shaking hands.

"Please eat, then go," said Mrs. Hirczi. She turned to Anna. *"Ich habe heute viel Erdbeeren gesammelt. Komm doch schnell wieder nach Hause. Wir haben viel Arbeit."* She disappeared around the side of the tent, where Janey had noticed a small work table and an open fire ringed by stones.

"Mama is not comfortable with English yet. But she says there are many strawberries in the tent. We can have some, but first, please help with these bottles. When we are finished, I take you and Mrs. Henderson's butter up to the main street."

Yeah, but then what, Janey wondered, hauling a crate to the side of the tent. How on earth was she going to find her way back into present-day Edmonton? She'd fallen into a hole and landed in a time zone with no guidebook to help her out.

Anna interrupted her thoughts. "Would you like to see the doll Papa and Mama gave me last Christmas?" she asked shyly.

Janey nodded, puzzled. What was an eleven-year-old doing getting a doll for Christmas? She followed Anna into the tent, which was divided into two rooms by a sheet hanging across the back. The scent from three baskets of strawberries, warmed from the sun's heat on the canvas, perfumed the flimsy structure.

The front room looked crowded but remarkably cosy, furnished with a rocking chair, benches, and several elaborately carved and painted wardrobes. At one of them, Anna pulled the bottom drawer open gently and carefully lifted a china doll from a bed of blankets. "This is Henrietta," she said tenderly, crooking the doll in her arm. "Her name, I think, sounds like the wind blowing soft in the springtime. It is a good name for her, no?"

The doll had a china face, blonde hair, and blue eyes the colour of a summer sky. "She's beautiful," said Janey solemnly, thinking of her own box full of dolls stashed away in her Toronto closet.

"Henrietta does not like to be alone for so long, but I do not like to take her in the wagon. She could fall and hurt herself. She looks very much like the doll I must leave in the Old Country." Anna stroked the china cheek tenderly.

"Back where I come from, girls our age don't play with dolls anymore," said Janey.

"Not at all?" Horrified, Anna clutched Henrietta to her chest.

"Well, yeah, when you're little, but by the time you're ten..." Once again the clash of shame and loyalty welled up inside her as she remembered sweeping her two favourite dolls from her bed when Becca and Rachel came to play.

"But that is terrible! Who do you sing to, or whisper your dreams or worries to at night?" asked Anna.

Brusquely, Janey changed the subject. "We'd better get Mrs. Henderson's butter to where it's going."

Anna tucked Henrietta back into the drawer and carefully closed it. "I wanted to call her Liesl, the name of my sister," she said softly, "but Mama said it would make her too sad."

As they got ready to leave, with pockets full of strawberries, Janey asked about a bathroom. "Oh, that is inside the tent," said Anna. "On Saturday nights."

It took a few seconds for Janey to understand. "No, not the bathroom. I meant the toilet. The...the...outhouse."

"Ah. That is at the very back, by the cliff. Be careful you do not go over!" Anna warned, emerging from the tent with what appeared to be a page torn from a catalogue and handing it to her.

Janey stared at the sheet, nonplussed. It had black-and-white drawings of little girls in ridiculously frilled dresses on it. "There is no paper in the privy," Anna explained.

Aha! Janey took the paper, and headed toward the cliff's edge, where a strange woman was just emerging from the outhouse. A little girl was waiting her turn, clutching a small sheet of newspaper, when Janey finished. Whoever invented toilet paper ought to get a medal, thought Janey as she climbed back into the wagon.

Once Rosa made it to the top of the hill, they turned onto Jasper Avenue, easing into a flow of wagons, horses, and pedestrians making their way along the wide, dusty road. Wooden storefronts selling everything from hardware and ladies hats to linens and legal advice lined the avenue. The planked sidewalks were crowded with men in suits or overalls and women in trailing skirts dragging straw-hatted girls and long-stockinged boys behind them.

"Where are we going?" Janey asked, finishing the strawberries. They were tinier than any she'd ever seen at a grocery store, but sweet and bursting with flavour.

"I must take the butter to the farmers' market, and then we will find your grandmother, yes? Where will we look?" Anna asked, as she handed her a thick slice of bread and some sausage.

How about ninety years down the road? thought Janey, wondering again how she could get out of her predicament. While Anna pulled up to an open area filled with stalls and produce, Janey swallowed a big bite of sausage and began, "Anna, look, I'm not really..." She paused in surprise when a short, round, Native woman, her black eyes alive in a face wrinkled with age, reached into the wagon and grabbed at Janey's skirt.

"You are not from here," said the old woman, giving Janey's dress a tug.

Anna jumped from the wagon and said cheerfully, "Good

RESCUE *at* FORT EDMONTON

afternoon, Mrs. Black Bear. This is Janey Kane and you are right, she is from the East." Anna tied Rosa to a post and dug the butter crate from its nest of straw.

"I'll be back soon," she called, already halfway through the stalls before Janey could even move from her seat. The woman still had a hold of her skirt.

"I know you. You are not from this time. You are looking for your home," said Mrs. Black Bear, drinking in Janey's face and hair. Janey nodded, stunned. Perhaps this old woman with the sharp eyes and round cheeks might know a way for her to return.

"I need to know how to get back," she said urgently. "Can you help me? Do you know the way?"

"You should not go back, but you must know more about what has happened," said Mrs. Black Bear. "You must go forward."

"Forward, backward, what's it matter? I need to get home. How do I get home?" Janey asked, becoming nervous under the woman's stare.

"You are asking the wrong questions," Mrs. Black Bear said carefully.

"The wrong questions! I've got nothing *but* questions! How on earth did I get here? Why am I here? What...ow!

Mrs. Black Bear stopped her by jabbing her finger in Janey's leg, exactly where Anna had pinched her. "Now you are asking the right question, girl. Why are you here?"

"I don't know," Janey wailed. "I didn't want to be here; I didn't want to be in Edmonton at either end of this century. I just want to be at home. I don't know why I'm in this

33

stupid place, stuck in this dumb dress, sitting on a wagon that's rattled loose every bone in my body..."

"I think," said Mrs. Black Bear, cutting Janey off, "that you are here to prevent a terrible thing. A disaster."

Janey stared at Mrs. Black Bear, letting the words sink in. "But how am I..."

"We will meet in another time. Remember the mines. It was good to see you again, Janey Kane." Mrs. Black Bear grinned and stepped into the crowds, the small white head lost in a sea of bowlers and straw hats.

Anna's elbow in her side brought Janey's attention back to the wagon. "I said, where do we go now? Where does your grandmother live? I hope it is not too far."

"Look Anna, I think I'm in way over my head. I think I'm lost."

Anna looked at Janey anxiously. "I think you really did hit your head. Those Jameson boys, they are a big trouble. Well, then, we will go back and help Mama with the bottles. Then, when Papa returns, he will know what to do," she said briskly, urging Rosa forward.

"What'll you do with those bottles?" asked Janey, glad to change the subject.

"We use them to keep food for winter. There are not enough jars for preserves – these days there are shortages of many things – but with the bottles you take off the top, I think you call it the neck, and then it is good. This morning I traded with the Henderson neighbours, bottles for coal."

As they neared the Hirczi tent, Anna frowned and urged Rosa to pick up some speed. Following Anna's gaze, Janey noticed a small crowd gathered in front of her friend's home.

"What you see here is the downfall of the Canadian West!" shouted one woman from the knot of oversized hats and long dresses. "No decent Christian home – not even the flimsy shelter of this poor woman here – is safe until the evils of alcohol are eliminated!" She stooped to pick up one of the bottles the girls had stacked earlier.

"Who are these women?" Janey asked as they pulled up to the tent.

"The Temperance Ladies – they hate liquor because it makes many men drunk," said Anna, jumping from the wagon.

The woman brandished the empty bottle. "Here, here is the evidence! How can these immigrants become productive members of our society when they are infected with Satan's drink? Look at the number of bottles here! Oh, for shame! For shame!" With a great heave, she flung the bottle over the side of the cliff.

"Stop! Stop! Do not do this!" cried Anna, rushing toward the crowd.

Anna's mother ran toward her daughter, crying. *"Anna, ich verstehe nicht! Was ist da los?"*

"We are the Woman's Christian Temperance Union and we will not stop until the evils of liquor are driven from our fair city," called another woman, reaching for a second bottle. A piercing whistle stopped her in mid-grab.

From the top of the wagon, Janey took her fingers from her mouth and sent a small prayer of thanks to her dad, who'd taught her how to whistle.

The group of women turned to her in surprise. "Now, just wait a minute," Janey called. "Why are you doing this?"

The crowd of elegantly-hatted females took in the tall, brown-haired girl in the ill-fitting blue dress with the straw hat hanging down her back. One of them stepped forward.

"Well. Who, may I ask, are you?" she demanded regally.

"I'm Janey Kane. Who are you?"

"My goodness, Janey Kane, where did they teach you your manners?" inquired the woman.

Not once had this woman answered her questions, thought Janey, as annoyance and the confusion of the day boiled up inside her. She'd had just about enough of everything.

"Where did they teach you *yours?* You can't just go around busting up people's property! You don't even know what they're using those bottles for! And you still haven't told me who you are."

"I am Mrs. Emily Murphy," said the woman, drawing herself up. "We are the ladies of the WCTU and we're here to eradicate the scourge of alcohol among these poor foreign families."

"Well, did you ask any questions before you went leaping to conclusions?" Janey demanded angrily, jumping off the wagon and approaching the crowd. "This family's using these bottles for canning. They're going to make strawberry jam."

Sheepishness crept across several of the women's faces, replacing their indignation. "Well, she should have used the King's own English and explained it to us!" said one of them, nodding at Mrs. Hirczi, who was clinging to Anna.

Now Janey was really furious. "That lady already speaks a whole other language. English is her second one," she said, advancing on the hapless woman. It was for moments such as these that Janey actually appreciated her height. "Just how many languages do *you* speak?" Janey was now nose to nose with the demonstrator, who seemed, suddenly, to find the sun unbearably hot.

Mrs. Murphy stepped between Janey and the woman. "Well, Janey Kane, you certainly know how to speak your mind." She studied her, then turned to the crowd.

"Ladies, I think our work here is finished. I believe we are needed at the beer parlour up the hill. We will rout evil at its source. Good afternoon, Janey Kane."

The knot of women picked up its skirts and marched out of the camp and up the hill. "Interesting girl, that Janey Kane," said Mrs. Murphy as she puffed up the steep incline. "Extremely headstrong, but that can be admirable in its own way. I'll remember that girl."

Once Anna explained the fuss to her mother, Mrs. Hirczi's worried face broke into a smile and she came over to hug Janey.

"You stay and eat with us dinner," she said. "But first..." she looked dejectedly at the bottles.

"Oh, Mama, Janey and I will finish these quickly," Anna said. She grabbed the crate and brought it to the work table behind the tent. Already, makeshift jars stood in the summer sunlight, filled with strawberry jam and covered with white cloth that appeared to be dipped in wax. A pot of jam simmered over the open fire.

"What are you dipping that string in?" asked Janey.

"Coal oil," explained Anna, as she tied the string around the bottle at the point where the glass bent to form the neck. She lit the string with a stick from the fire, then plunged the bottle into a bucket of water beside her. The string sizzled and the bottle snapped, exactly where the string had been.

"That's so cool!" said Janey.

"No, the string is hot and the water is cold. That makes the glass break," explained Anna. The girls worked together in the late afternoon sun, while Mrs. Hirczi put potatoes on the fire and placed sausages in a cast-iron frying pan.

Two figures separated themselves from the throng of people moving past on the road and walked toward the tent, casting long shadows behind them. "Peter! Papa! You're home!" cried Anna, rushing toward them. Her excited tale of the day's events, babbled in a mixture of English and German, perked up the grimy, tired-looking figures. She introduced her new friend and then urged her father and brother toward the wash basin.

"Can you fill this with water from the bucket by the fire?" she asked Janey, handing her a pitcher.

Afterwards, Janey never really could figure out what had happened, but decided her dress had somehow swept too close to the fire. As she brushed by the tent, she heard a crackle but ignored it. Only when she felt the prickle of heat against her legs did she look down and realize her dress was burning.

Janey leapt away from the table, shouting, "Fire! Fire!"

Mr. Hirczi came running with the water from the basin. But instead of pouring it on her, he dashed it against the tent. Beating off the tiny, licking flames on her skirt, Janey realized to her horror that the Hirczis' home was burning up.

A flaming hole was also spreading on the side of her dress. She ran past people from neighbouring camps carrying gunny sacks, buckets, and bowls of water, and flung herself on a patch of ground, hoping to smother the flames on her dress.

Finally, when she was sure her clothes were no longer burning, she sat up and looked at the Hirczi camp. The fire was out, but the tent was a smouldering mass of sodden canvas, draped over awkward bits of furniture. Men from neighbouring camps were stamping out glowing embers, while kerchiefed women gathered around a stunned-looking Mrs. Hirczi.

What have I done? thought Janey. Suddenly, Anna's voice pierced the air. "Henrietta! My Henrietta!" she called and Janey watched as Anna rushed toward the ruins.

Horrified, Janey got up and backed away from the sight of Anna desperately ploughing through the dripping canvas. This is all my fault, she thought. I should have been more careful! I've just ruined their home! Her head ringing with accusations, Janey turned from the scene and ran blindly in the opposite direction.

The burned dress only hampered her escape, and Janey paused to rip the thing off so she could flee even faster. That old woman was wrong. I can't stop terrible things from happening. I make them happen. This is horri...

Janey's mind went blank as she plunged over the side of the riverbank. She'd forgotten Anna's warning, and now she was tumbling, falling, head over heels down the side of a clay bank that scraped her back and legs.

When she finally stopped rolling, she lay on the cool earth with her eyes closed and tried to catch her breath. She should have left the dress on. It would have spared her some scratches.

"Janey. Janey! Janey, for pity's sake will you get yourself out of there! You're not supposed to be in there."

Janey opened her eyes. Her grandmother was standing on the other side of a construction fence, worry creasing the lines around her eyes.

CHAPTER THREE

S TIFF AND SORE, JANEY SAT UP. THERE, GLINTING MOCK-
ingly in the muck, lay Granny's locket, part of its chain
draped casually over her now filthy sneakers. She
stared at it in a daze.

"Janey! Janey!?! What *is* the matter with you? Will you
get yourself out of there this instant?" Granny's voice had an
uncharacteristically sharp edge to it.

"I'm, uh...I'm coming," said Janey, reaching for the
necklace. The chain rolled off her foot and she felt the earth
rumble beneath her. She lunged for the locket and the
tremors stopped. Getting to her feet, she looked quickly
around the site. No gaping holes; no collapsed earth anywhere around her. Nothing to indicate she'd just dropped
through metres of earth and decades of time into another
era. Janey checked her watch. That's odd, she thought; it
seemed to be working again.

She ambled over to the fence and, with an ungraceful leap, landed beside her grandmother.

"You look as if you've fought with a mud monster and lost," said Granny, trying to keep her irritation in check. The sight of her granddaughter lying sprawled in the mud had unnerved her. "What on earth were you doing there?"

"I accidentally...no, the locket accidentally fell in," said Janey. "And I jumped over to get it." She paused, wondering if she should tell her grandmother the rest of it.

"It looked like you'd decided to have a nap in there," said Granny. "A construction site is not the first place I'd think of for a lie-down."

"Fine then! The next time the necklace flies off to some weird place, I'll just leave it there," Janey snapped. Scowling, she stomped up the wooden sidewalk and headed toward the park's main gate, trying desperately to sort out what had just happened to her. Or might have happened to her. Or maybe hadn't happened to her at all.

"Oh, Janey, for heaven's sake. Stop making heavy weather about everything. And slow down! I can't keep up with you if you're racing off like this."

"The creeps? What on earth for? The stuff around here is just a little old," said Granny, catching up. "Like me."

Janey knew an olive branch of peace when she heard one. "You're not *that* old, Granny," she said, slowing her pace to accommodate her grandmother, who was breathing rather heavily. "I'm just tired from the trip, and the time change and everything. And I think I must have pulled a muscle when I jumped over that fence. So much for being the track and field star in junior high."

"You ought to play basketball," said Granny. "That's what I did when I was young, and about as tall as you. I was pretty good. I even played on the farm team for the Edmonton Grads. They travelled all over the world. Maybe when we get home I could show you –"

Hot, grubby, and tired, Janey cut her off. "The only thing I want to do when we get home is take a bath."

THE WATER IN GRANNY'S CLAW-FOOT TUB was steaming when Janey climbed in. She leaned back and closed her eyes, letting the heat do its work on her body while she sorted out what had happened. There was no way she'd just imagined the events of today, Janey thought. Her muscles *felt* as if she'd plummeted down a deep hole and then crawled out into a world of rock-pelting pinheads and bone-rattling wagon rides. She lifted one leg from the water and examined it. Bruises all over the place. That one must have come when she fell over the cliff and that one, there, wasn't that just where Anna and that weird woman poked her?

Her leg flopped back into the water. Who was she kidding? There was no way she'd really fallen back into a time almost a hundred years ago. She wished she could tell someone, talk to someone about it. Granny might listen to her, but she'd probably think Janey was making the whole thing up.

But that anguished cry from Anna, as she tried to get

back to the tent – that all seemed so real. Janey could hear Anna's desperate shriek again and again in her mind. What were they doing now? Where would they sleep tonight? And Anna's doll – in that tiny tent it was probably the only thing other than her clothes that Anna owned. A wave of guilt washed over Janey.

Maybe Janey was just sick, coming down with something, and the whole thing was a feverish dream. She removed her hand from the steaming water and felt her head. Naw. It was cooler than her pruney fingers at the moment.

"Janey, are the clothes you had on in there with you? I thought I'd throw them in the wash," Granny called through the door.

"They're on the rug in my room," said Janey, working shampoo through her hair.

Her dad had promised to come out soon; maybe he could fly out this weekend. Then he could help her sort it out. If there really was anything to sort out.

But the whole thing had seemed so real, Janey thought, lying back so her hair floated in a soft billow around her head. She could still taste the tang of that buttermilk in the back of her throat, and the incredible sweetness of those tiny wild strawberries. She and Granny had stopped to pick up groceries on the way home and Janey'd convinced her grandmother to buy some buttermilk. But it hadn't tasted quite the same.

"Where's buttermilk come from, Granny?" Janey had asked, as she helped with the supper dishes.

"It's the stuff that's left over inside the churn after they make the butter," said Granny, pausing to catch her breath as she scoured out the sink. "I used to date a dairy farmer," she said, grinning. "Well, the son of a dairy farmer."

"You mean, not Grampa?"

"Of course not Grampa. He was petrified of large animals, especially cows. Had a thing about them. Funny, really. We were at a farm once and he accidentally wandered into a field with a whole herd of them. Stood there so terrified I had to get the farmer to shoo them away. Your father never seemed to like them much either."

Well, that certainly explained her own thing about cows, thought Janey, swishing her hair back and forth underwater and pretending she was one of those models in a shampoo commercial. "As if," Janey muttered out loud. "Get a grip, girl," she told herself, sitting up to slop on some citrus-scented conditioner.

That was the other thing she'd noticed, she realized. The whole time she'd been in that "other time," she'd smelled all this weird stuff. Like horse manure and chicken poop and even, under the scent of the flowery perfumes those temperance women wore, the sharp smell of sweat. I'll bet not one of those hoity-toity ladies had ever seen a stick of deodorant, Janey thought as she climbed out of the tub. How could she have made up those smells?

Granny was on the phone when Janey emerged from the bathroom in clean shorts and t-shirt. "Hold on, Alex, she's finished her beauty regimen. I think she can talk to you now." The older woman could barely move aside fast enough before Janey grabbed the phone.

"Hi, Daddy!"

"Hi, sweetie. So. How was your first day in the Wild West?"

Janey paused. What could she tell him about today? The truth? What was the truth? Would he believe her?

"Dad, you gotta come out. I need to talk to you."

"Whoa! You miss me that much after just one day? I'm touched. Really. And not just in the head."

"Daddy, stop kidding. When are you coming out? Can you come this weekend?"

"I don't think so, honey. In fact, the meeting I thought I'd be at in a couple of weeks has been delayed. It looks as if I won't be able to see your beaming smile till August."

"August! But that's, like, months away! Why can't you come out earlier? You promised." She dropped her voice. "Besides, this place is just too weird for me. I don't like it. And I miss everyone back there. I want to come home."

"Janey, there's nothing weird about Granny or her house. She may be sick, but I think she's holding together pretty well," her father said sharply.

"Granny's sick?"

In the silence that followed, Janey thought she could hear her blood pounding against the receiver, then her father's sigh. "I thought she'd told you yesterday," he said. "Granny's been having treatments for cancer. She says she's fine, but I thought you could keep an eye on her for me over the summer."

"So you just send me out here and don't tell me any of this?"

"Well, I wasn't quite sure how to do it. And we thought Granny might want to tell you herself."

"Well, she hasn't," said Janey, her voice rising. "And now while you guys are having a great time in Toronto and Turkey, I'm stuck out here? This is so unfair. Why do I have to do your dirty work?"

"Honey..."

"I'm not your stupid honey. I hate you. I don't care if you don't come!" Janey smashed down the phone, turned, and saw Granny standing in the doorway.

"Hey, kiddo..."

"Just leave me alone. I don't want anything to do with some old sick woman!" Janey yelled, and instantly regretted it as she saw her grandmother's face. Horrified, she put her hand to her mouth. Then, for the second time that day, she fled the scene of a disaster.

THE LANE BEHIND HER GRANDMOTHER'S HOUSE ended with a stand of trees, dressed in the bright green leaves of early summer. But Janey hardly noticed; she was just running blindly toward the cool dark shade beneath.

Why, oh why, couldn't she just keep her mouth shut? And why hadn't anyone told her that Granny was sick? And why had she said such horrible things? That last question churned up the guilty knot already growing in her stomach.

She plunged into the cool darkness of the trees and realized she was heading downhill toward a ravine. Wait a minute, she thought, clutching a thin poplar tree to stop her

RITA FEUTL

descent. I'm not being thrown into some weird time warp again. Especially now that I've just had a bath.

Janey stepped gingerly forward. Nothing happened. Assured of her footing, she continued downhill, and noticed a path past a row of scraggly bushes. Reaching it, she waited for a cyclist to zip by (modern helmet, she noticed, and at least twenty gears; definitely present-day) before she followed.

Joggers and dog walkers ambled or zipped past while Janey tried to put her thoughts in order. No wonder Granny's hair was so blonde. She'd bet anything it was a wig. She'd heard about this cancer stuff. Wasn't that what Rachel's bossy grandmother died of? Rachel had missed more than a week of school, and Janey could still remember her friend complaining about how dumb the wig had looked on her grandmother as she lay in the coffin.

Janey's eyes misted over. This was all so stupid. Her own granny drove a cool car and wasn't bossy and had had a whole life with boyfriends and everything, stuff Janey was only starting to know about.

Everything was so unfair. Why hadn't her parents told her about Granny being sick? And why did she have to be the one to deal with it?

Her blind rambling was interrupted when a golden retriever puppy loped toward her, tongue lolling. Without thinking, Janey stooped to pat it and the tears overflowed, dripping on the animal's muzzle. It snuffled up and licked the rest off Janey's face, until Janey was half crying, half laughing, on the pavement.

"Sammy! Sammy! Get down, girl! Stop that!"

A dark-haired boy in a ripped pair of jeans grabbed the back of the dog's collar and yanked her back. "Sorry about that. Sam's just a bit over-friendly."

"It's okay. Really. She's cute." Janey got to her feet, wiping tears from her face, hoping he'd think it was just dog slobber. But before her eyes were dry, the wiping had changed to batting. It was only now that Janey realized a cloud of mosquitoes had gathered around her.

"Man, these bugs are vicious," she said, swatting away frantically.

A grin spread on the boy's face. "You can't be from around here. You oughtta know that if you go into the ravine just before the sun goes down, you've gotta be bug-proofed."

Janey eyed him through the swatting. "You're right. I'm not. What's your secret?"

"Piles of bug spray. My mum says it's full of cancer stuff, but she doesn't walk the dog down here at dusk."

At the mention of cancer, the small lift of Janey's spirits collapsed again. She glanced around, thinking she'd go home and face the music, then realized she wasn't sure of where she was or how to get back. "Look, I think I'm lost. How do you get out of here?"

"Where're ya going?"

"Uh, yeah. To my grandmother. She lives at...ummm, I mean... Oh no." Great, she thought. I'm standing here like a fool slapping myself silly and I don't have a hot clue where I'm going. He must think I'm a dork.

"What's her name?"

"Whose? My grandmother's?"

"Well, I'd ask you for yours, but you're a little confused at the moment..."

Janey stopped swatting for a second and eyed him. What did he mean, confused? Who did he think he was? "I'm Janey Kane, and my grandmother's..."

"Old Mrs. Kane, right next to my piano teacher! I know who you are. My mum knows her. She said her granddaughter was coming out."

"So who are you?"

"I'm Mike. Mike Wegner. We live a few avenues away from you."

"Well, Mike, can you show me the way up and out? If I stay here, I'm going to be devoured."

"Sure. Your grandma makes the best popcorn cake. You should ask her to make it for you. How's she doin' anyhow?"

"What do you mean?" asked Janey, following Mike and Sammy out of the ravine.

"I know she's been sick. My mum's been over a few times. And I know your dad was out a few months back."

Great, thought Janey. The whole world knows Granny's been sick except for me. "Yeah. She's supposed to be better now. I'm kinda out here to help her."

Janey hadn't even noticed they'd stopped in front of Granny's house until the screen door opened. "There you are, Janey. Oh, you've met Michael. How's your mum, dear?"

"She's fine, Mrs. Kane. Are you gonna make Janey your popcorn cake?"

Granny grinned. "When I do, we'll have you over for some, okay?"

"It's a deal. I've gotta go. Sammy's desperate for the rest of her walk."

He raised a hand to Janey and then headed toward the ravine. Janey turned up the path.

"Granny, I'm sorry."

Granny came down the stairs and hugged her. "You didn't know, kiddo, and it's awful having news like that sprung on you. It's been my fault, really. I've been a bit of a coward." She released Janey and lowered herself on to the stair. "I asked your parents not to tell you, and then I wasn't quite sure when I should."

The light from the porch fell on Granny's upturned face, harshly accentuating the tiny lines radiating from her eyes and mouth. She's old, Janey realized, as a wave of emotion swept over her. She sat down beside her grandmother and gave her a squeeze.

"It's all right," said Janey. "I don't suppose there is a right time for anything like that. Are you okay? What's happening with you?"

"Well, I'm finished my treatments and I have another appointment at the end of the week. I felt pretty crummy last winter and spring, but your dad's visit helped. And now things seem to be better. Except for my hair, of course." She looked at Janey. "Did you guess it was a wig?"

"Granny, I really, really thought it was your own hair. And it looks pretty good on you. In fact, I kinda thought you were, you know, looking for a new husband."

Granny's roar of laughter could probably be heard clear across the ravine, Janey thought. "Me? A husband? In this state?" She wiped tears from her eyes.

"Oh, kiddo. I knew you'd be the best thing for me. That's why I didn't want your parents out here, hovering over me as if I was going to keel over the next instant." She was still chuckling when Mike and Sammy strolled by in the darkness.

"Aren't you two getting eaten by the bugs?" Mike called out.

Janey stood up suddenly. I can't believe it, she thought. I'm only here for a day and I'm already sitting out on the front stoop in the evening. She hoped the tinkling she heard was from Sammy's collar, and not some dumb cowbell in the distance.

As Janey pulled the quilt off her bed that night, an avalanche of tiny items clattered to the floor. Amidst the coins and candies was a crumpled ticket to the historical park. Granny must have emptied the pockets of her shorts before she put them in the wash.

But when Janey reached under the dresser to pick up the last object, goosebumps crawled up her arm. A small, bone-white button, perfect for a pinafore, lay in her hand – the one Anna had given her to keep on the wagon ride.

It was true! She had been back! She hadn't dreamt the whole thing, thought Janey, clutching the proof in her hand as she slipped into bed.

What had that old woman said? That she was supposed to stop a disaster? Well, she certainly hadn't stopped anything today. About the only thing she'd prevented was having her grandmother hate her totally for calling her a sick old woman.

Maybe the thing she was supposed to prevent was in the past, thought Janey. What's-her-name...Mrs. Black Bear... hadn't she said something about meeting again? But how?

And she'd said something about remembering the mines. What mines? Janey hadn't run into any mines around here. Mines were supposed to be underground and she hadn't... wait a minute! The construction site! Maybe it was on top of an old mine like the one Anna's dad worked at – maybe that's what those tunnels were!

But Janey's excitement quickly died out. Jump back into that sinkhole again? Risk being smothered and slimed? Maybe she should just ignore the whole thing. Forget about it. After all, what could one twelve-year-old girl do to stop something bad from happening? Not much.

Janey stuffed the button under her pillow. The last image in her mind before she drifted into an uneasy sleep was of Anna, carefully cradling her china doll.

STUMBLING FROM HER BEDROOM the next morning, Janey was jolted awake by the sight of her grandmother sitting at the table with a kerchief wrapped around an otherwise bald head.

"Oh Granny..." She paused, dumbfounded.

"You're supposed to say, 'What big ears you have,'" said her grandmother, grinning at Janey over the rim of her teacup.

"It's actually not the ears – they're fine," said Janey, coming closer. "But you have no eyebrows."

"It's true, it's true. There's not a single hair on my head. Yet."

Janey studied her grandmother's face. "How come I didn't notice the eyebrow thing yesterday?"

"It's amazing, the stuff they teach you to do with make-up. I think I might be able to take you up on last night's suggestion and find myself a husband yet."

"Yeah? So where are you looking?" Janey sat down across from her and poured cereal into a bowl.

"Here and there. I turn a lot of heads when I'm out with Marilyn, you know."

"I bet you do. How about we take Marilyn out today, say maybe over to that big mall with all the cool stuff inside it?"

The look of amusement in Granny's eyes dimmed. "I don't think so, kiddo. I'm afraid yesterday took a bit out of me. Today will have to be a quiet day."

Janey pushed the flash of disappointment away. Of course. She couldn't be dragging her sick grandmother all over the city. But what was she supposed to do? "You could always spend the day down at the pool," said Granny. "Give Michael a call and see what he's up to."

Call up a strange boy? She HAD to be kidding. "Maybe I'll just spend the day reading. I brought a lot of books along."

SEVERAL QUIET DAYS FOLLOWED. Janey read, watched TV, and gently took the hoe from Granny when she caught her out in her garden. Together they planted a row of sunflowers. By the second day, Janey figured Granny cheated at gin rummy, but couldn't grasp exactly how. She managed to catch Becca one night on the telephone. Her pal assured Janey that life in Toronto was just as boring for her at the moment. Janey didn't tell her about Anna and her tent and her doll.

One morning, as Janey headed into the backyard with a book, Granny suggested she haul down the lounge chairs from the garage rafters. "Just don't kill yourself on any of the other stuff in there."

The garage smelled of weathered wood and packed dirt floors. Marilyn sat regally in one half, but the other side was stuffed with an old stove, an ancient one-speed bicycle, a push mower, and various garden implements. Janey found a rickety ladder and set it under the rafters where the lounge chairs were stored. As she pulled them toward her, she caught sight of a spattered blue trunk under the eaves. "Hey, Granny," she bellowed through the side door. "What's in here?"

"Just stuff that belonged to your grandfather," said Granny, coming into the shadows of the garage. "Funny. I'd forgotten about that thing. It's been parked up there for decades. Be careful, kiddo. There can't be anything in there worth breaking your neck over."

Janey was already yanking the trunk toward her. "How can you have this here and not know what's in it?"

"Did I say I'd forgotten? Really, my dear..." Granny's voice dropped as she stepped close to the ladder, "you're about to uncover the deepest, darkest of our family secrets. When your grandfather was young he was...a great train robber. That's where we kept the gold and stolen jewellery."

"Stop teasing, Granny," said Janey. Still, she couldn't help the tiny surge of excitement that raced through her as she dragged the trunk into the garden and lifted the lid.

Naturally, the disappointment was twice as big. Nothing but clothes – an old blue jacket with brass buttons down the front, some overalls, and a soft flannel shirt. About the only thing of real value was a silky white scarf. Big deal, thought Janey. Why would anyone want to save this stuff?

Granny pulled the jacket out. "I can't say I remember Grampa wearing this pea coat; he was a much bigger man. I'm not sure why he had it packed away."

Overcoming her disappointment, Janey slipped into the jacket, which hung, overlarge, on her shoulders. She put her hands on her hips and sashayed down the garden path. "For the well-dressed man of the season, this coat has everything," she said, swivelling her hips wildly in imitation of a model.

There were snickers from the back gate. "Guess that means I'll have to have one," said a voice. Janey froze, clutching the coat around her. Mike's eyes were on her, as were those of a girl just a little taller than him, who grinned at Janey.

"Hi, Michael," said Granny. "And is that Nicky with you? Come on in, you two."

If ever there was a time when the ground *should* have opened up and swallowed her, it was now, thought Janey.

How embarrassing. She stuck her hands into the jacket pockets and pulled it around her, trying to hide.

"Hi, Mrs. Kane. We were wondering if Janey wanted to go to the pool with us."

"I, uh, um." She felt something crackle and drew her hand out. In it were several folded sheets of newsprint with pictures on them. They looked strangely familiar, like... exactly like the paper Anna had given her yesterday for the outhouse. She stared at the pages, entranced.

"Janey?" Her grandmother looked at her quizzically.

"What? Oh. Yeah. Um. Thanks, Mike. But I think I'm going to spend some time with my granny right now..."

"Sweetheart, you don't have to..."

"It's okay, Granny. But maybe tomorrow." She looked at Mike. "Thanks."

"It'll probably be hot tomorrow too," said Mike, turning away. "C'mon, Nickster." Janey hardly noticed the girl's narrowing eyes, or the pair's departure. She was staring at a page of china dolls and prices. One of them looked remarkably like Anna's doll, Henrietta. Guilt laid its clammy hand on her again, but with it, came an idea. What if Janey just went back to buy Anna a new doll? Even if she didn't complete her mission about a disaster, at least she wouldn't feel so guilty.

"Granny, is it very far to Fort Edmonton?"

"Well, no, not that far, but –"

"Could you please take me there again? You don't even have to come with me. You could just drop me there. I didn't get to see everything when I was there with you."

"But sweetheart! I just got myself settled..."

"All right then. This afternoon. Or could I take the bike in the garage?"

"Oh, I don't think I want you racing through the city on your own. What would your parents say?"

"Oh, but Granny, it'd be fun! And I'd get some exercise and everything." The exercise thing always worked with her mother.

"I don't think I can let you go on your own." Granny watched the disappointment register on her granddaughter's face. "How about this. After lunch, I'll drive you over and then meet you again at five o'clock at the gate. But don't go having naps in any construction sites, okay?"

JANEY CAREFULLY CONSIDERED HER WARDROBE. Back in Toronto, she hadn't really packed for sliding down sinkholes; nor was anything she had suitable for wearing in 1907. Hanging next to an ancient, scratchy, black-and-gold basketball uniform at the back of the closet was Janey's one dress. A sleeveless number that ended above the knee, it would probably make the Mrs. Hendersons or Mrs. Mur-phys of the time pop a gasket. Janey smiled at the thought, but realized she had nothing in her closet that a girl of almost a century ago could wear strolling down Edmonton's boardwalks.

But there was no way she was going to borrow some other girl's dress and apron and – oh, man – stockings. Boys had it so much easier. They just put on pants and a shirt and off they went. Simple.

Indignant, Janey's eyes roamed over her wardrobe, and

rested on her own pants, which consisted of two pairs of jeans. Well...? Why shouldn't she wear jeans, and just go as a boy? Anna would freak, but Janey could handle her. And it would make it so much easier to wander through the crowds.

But as she eyed her choices, Janey realized both her pairs of jeans were too tight, too decorated, and just too modern looking. What she needed was an old, baggy, inconspicuous pair that a little (or a lot) of muck wouldn't hurt.

Grampa's overalls! She dashed out to the garage and pulled them out, as well as the flannel shirt, and even, oh joy, a kind of a cap she was sure she'd seen Anna's brother wearing. Back in her bedroom, she tried on her costume, tucking her hair under the cap. She inspected herself critically in the mirror. Not bad. She could pass for a friend of Peter's. The shirt's collar buttoned high enough that you'd never even notice the silver chain of Granny's locket. She changed back into shorts and a top and tucked her wardrobe into a backpack.

"I'm ready whenever you are, Granny."

ONCE JANEY WAS THROUGH THE PARK GATE, she found a washroom and pulled her costume on over her clothes. The pinafore button and the money for Anna's doll tucked safely in her pocket, she checked her watch. She had four hours to rush into the past, find Anna, buy her a new doll, save the world, and get back. Realizing her cap wouldn't stay on her head while she tumbled into the past, Janey stuffed it into her overalls.

She made her way to the construction site, stashed her backpack by a fencepost and, when no one was looking, jumped over the fence. It was awkward with the extra clothing, and Janey stumbled as she landed. It didn't help that she was trying to keep her hands clasped protectively over her face.

Nothing happened.

She crouched, waiting. Not a tremor, not a movement. Cautiously, she removed her hands. Maybe she'd landed at the wrong place? She climbed back out, studied the fence and leaped again. Still nothing.

Janey straightened. Wonderful. Now what? How was she going to get to the mine if she couldn't get under the earth? Was she supposed to dig her way through the decades? And with what? She hadn't thought to bring a shovel. Maybe she *had* invented the whole thing in her head.

Granny's locket swayed against her as she moved back to the fence. Janey paused, trying to remember something. She peered at the dirt, noticing that it wasn't as muddy as it had been several days earlier. But there was something else...to do with the locket. When Granny woke her up the last time, Janey remembered, she had moved her foot and the chain had rolled off her leg and the earth...had shifted.

That was it! The locket! She had to let go of the locket! Janey dug the chain out from under the coveralls, and pulled it off her head. Briefly she watched the silver ornament sway in the sunshine, then stretched out her arm and dropped it onto the dirt.

Instantly, the ground started shaking. Janey hardly had a chance to cover her face before the earth swallowed her up.

CHAPTER FOUR

I T SEEMED TO JANEY THAT THE PLUMMETING, SUFFO-
cating feeling didn't last nearly as long this time, perhaps
because she wasn't quite so terrified. But when her body
stopped sliding and the earth settled around her, she pulled
herself out of the mini-landslide and felt like smacking herself. Why hadn't she thought to bring a flashlight? She fumbled for her watch and breathed a sigh of relief when its
small glow fought back the darkness.

There were the tunnels; three dark and dank passageways
heading off in different directions. But which one would get
her back to Anna? The last time...yes, the last time a light
had led her to the girl. Janey released her watch and waited
for her eyes to adjust to the dark. A faint, comforting
glimmer pointed Janey to the tunnel on her left.

The extra layer of overalls must have given her added

padding, thought Janey grimly, because the passageway seemed narrower and harder to negotiate than before. She was hot and sweaty by the time she reached the opening, but she yanked her cap out of her pocket and jammed it down over her head. No sense letting those stupid Jameson boys take advantage of her again.

Reaching sunlight, the dank, earthy smell gave way to a mellow, dusty scent of leaves long past the vibrant pulse of early summer. Janey caught sight of a stand of poplar, blazing yellow against the blue of the prairie sky, and realized that even if she hadn't fallen back into history, she'd at least time-shifted a whole season. She squirmed out of the hole and got to her feet.

Instantly, something heavy crashed against her back and pitched her forward. The sound of an explosion rocked the air behind her and something whistled over her head.

"Well, if that don't beat all! I missed her!" a rough, angry voice shouted out. "Who was that idiot?"

A younger voice, right above Janey, scolded in whispers into her ear. "Crazy! You are crazy! You shouldn't be here." Janey couldn't agree more, but the words wouldn't come out. Winded from the fall, she was being squashed against the ground by a solid weight. She groaned and the weight moved. Janey rolled over and her cap spilled off.

"But...you're a girl!" said the owner of the young voice, a small, nut-brown child of about seven who examined Janey with dark, puzzled eyes. Janey grabbed her cap.

"Louisa! Louisa! Come here!" From across the clearing, another voice, female, sounded both anxious and annoyed.

"Uh, yes, Mama. One minute!" the little girl called over

her shoulder. She grabbed a startled Janey by the hand and yanked her into the brush.

"Louisa!" repeated the voice. Another explosion went off, slightly further away.

"Yes, Mama!" Louisa called again, then turned sharply to a bewildered Janey. "Everyone knows not to get in the way of the hunters! Are you crazy? You can't be from here. Who *are* you? Where are you from?"

Ears ringing from the explosions and the persistent questions, Janey could hardly frame a response. "I, uh, you're right. I'm sorry, I didn't know..."

The vague, bewildered answers didn't satisfy the girl. She stared closely at Janey, stuck her finger in her mouth, then rubbed it on Janey's cheek.

"Eww. Yuck! Don't rub your..."

"But...you are white – like my father!" said Louisa, awestruck. "You are a girl and you are white like, like, the belly of a fish!"

Oh sure, thought Janey. I listen to my mother and slather on the sunscreen and what do I get for it? Fish belly skin. "Look," she said, sighing, "I'm not from here; I'm from the East..."

"Louisa! Come. Now!" demanded the irritated voice in the distance.

"We'd better go to Mama," said Louisa. "She'll know what to do with you." Motioning Janey to follow, she scooted through the brush that circled the open field. Another explosion urged Janey to keep close to Louisa's heels. When they'd gone halfway around, the child called out softly: "Mama! I'm here! Come see!"

A short, round figure carrying a large basket came toward the little girl. The woman wore a long black skirt and a loose cotton blouse, brightened by an intricately beaded leather belt at the waist and a red kerchief around the neck.

"When I call you, Louisa, you must come! It is foolish to wander those fields when the men are out hunting. Martin is furious that he missed that doe," scolded the woman, her heavy black braids swaying as she walked toward them.

"But Mama, look what I've found," said the girl, skipping to the side to let her mother take in Janey.

The woman stopped and stared. Then she reached forward and grabbed Janey's face, turning her chin from one side to another. She, too, rubbed at some of the tunnel dirt from Janey's cheeks.

"Ow!" said Janey, shoving the woman's hands away. "Get your hands off me."

"She is from the East, Mama. And she is a girl."

"She is trouble," said the woman, taking a step back from Janey.

"I don't want to be any trouble," said Janey hastily. "I'm looking for a girl called Anna. She lives with her family in a tent along the riverbank, below where the town is. Actually, her tent might have burned down during the summer. But if you'll just point me in the right direction, I'll leave you here..."

Louisa frowned and shook her head. "No girls with English names live in tents this year. And none of the tents have burned down." She grabbed Janey's hand. "We don't live in a tent. We live at Edmonton House. My Papa, Mr. Fisher, gave me my name, and my Grandpapa, Mr. King, who died a terrible, terrible death, gave my..."

"Louisa! That tongue in your head flaps like a tent opening on a windy day! It is nothing but trouble. Be still!" Mrs. Fisher turned to Janey. "And you. You are even bigger trouble. Why are you here? There are no white women at Edmonton House..."

"I'm not really sure why I'm here. Well, yes, I am...well, partly. I need to make it up to Anna, but I think I'm supposed to do something else, stop something...terrible..." Janey's voice petered out as the woman's eyes bore into her, studying her.

"Mama has magical powers," said Louisa, sidling up to Janey again. "She can see with her dreams..."

"Louisa! Go and get your basket. Do NOT get in the way of the hunters and do NOT say a word about this." Another explosion crackled in the distance. The woman nodded at Janey. "You must go back. There is nothing for you here. There is no town, no girl called Anna. No towns for many, many days. You are in the wrong place. There is only Edmonton House."

Janey's heart sank. "Just one house?"

"It is not just a house. It is the fort – the Hudson's Bay Company fort. It is very big."

Janey was puzzled. She was sure she'd seen more than that when she'd crossed the river with Anna. There'd been stores and shops and sidewalks... A suspicion snuck up on her. "Is this 1907?"

"What do you mean?"

"Is this the year, I mean...what year are we in?"

A spark of pity flashed across Mrs. Fisher's face. "Reverend Rundle starts many of his sermons with 'In this year of our Lord, 1846.'" She watched the girl's smudged face crumple.

"I've come back to the wrong time..." whispered Janey, almost to herself.

"Then turn around. Go back," said Mrs. Fisher sharply.

A male figure stomped down the path toward them. "Mrs. Fisher, if you can't tell your brat not to get in my way and prattle on with foolish tales, I'll whop her so hard her tongue'll roll right out of her head."

Before Janey could quite figure out what was happening, the woman whipped her kerchief from her neck and tied it, pirate-style, around Janey's head.

"Here boy, you lazy creature!" said Mrs. Fisher loudly, staring at Janey with a mixture of belligerence and warning. "No rosehips grow here. Stop hiding and do some real work."

"And who's this now, Mrs. Fisher?" The boy, a pimple-faced sixteen-year-old with greasy brown hair covered in a kerchief like Janey's, peered around Mrs. Fisher's stout form.

"He is with that party from Rocky Mountain House. They are waiting for the York boats to come in."

"I don't remember no boy," said the other suspiciously. "What's your name then?"

"Ja...James. Friends call me Jamey," said Janey, taking her cues from Mrs. Fisher. Being a boy was obviously the better choice at the moment.

"Enough of all this talking and wasting time," said Mrs. Fisher, brushing past the other boy. "Have you two nothing better to do than stand here and talk? You're both as bad as my Louisa."

"Now, Mrs. Fisher, I just came over to ask you to help me with this doe I took down."

Mrs. Fisher nodded in Janey's direction. "Well, Martin, here are idle hands begging for work."

JANEY HAD NEVER BEEN the wild woodswoman type. She preferred to do her hunting in the sales racks of cosmetic shops and clothing stores. And any raw meat she'd ever dealt with had come wrapped in plastic and Styrofoam from a grocery store.

So when she saw the caramel-coloured deer lying in the yellow stubble near a stand of firs across the field, she looked away again quickly. Maybe she could find the tunnel she'd just used. If she was quick, she could just slip off and try another. But where had she come up?

"Did you hide in that tunnel to shoot the deer?" asked Janey in what she hoped was a casual tone. Hoping to appear more boyish, she shoved her hands in her pockets. It occurred to her that the money she'd tucked in there to buy Anna a new doll had disappeared. Great, thought Janey, rooting through each hidey-hole on her overalls.

"What tunnel?" Martin was looking at her as if she'd lost her mind.

"You know, a deep hole that seems to go on forever," said Janey, giving up on the money and studying the terrain around her.

"I been livin' here for a year now and I ain't seen no tunnel on this field to hide in." They reached the deer and Janey could feel her stomach pitch. "Leastways, there's nothin' here that would hide the size of you if you were tryin' to avoid the work God gave ya."

The deer was a crumpled mass of fur and hoofs and unseeing, glassy eyes staring into the fall sky. Janey didn't know whether the cold that gripped her was from the sight of the dead doe, or from the creeping afternoon shadows spreading across the field. Martin pulled out the knife at his waist and drew the blade across the animal's throat. Blood gushed from the wound and Janey forced a scream back down her own throat.

"Well, don't just stand there," said Martin. "Help me get her onto that slope." Janey touched the slender hind legs, still warm in the autumn sunshine. Martin was already dragging the body toward an incline, the head hanging at an odd angle as blood pulsed from the gash beneath it.

"If ya pick the creature up, we can be back before winter," snapped Martin. She grasped the legs, and helped him heave the body up and over to the slope. Martin arranged it so the blood drained downhill and then stood back. "Biggest one yet this year," he said, with a hint of pride in his voice. "It'll feed a lot of the families."

Janey looked everywhere but at the dead animal at her feet. How could you make small talk while this was happening right in front of you? How could she get out of here? Why hadn't she thought about how she was supposed to get back before she pitched herself into the past?

"Now grab the legs again and put her on her back," Martin ordered. She reached for them awkwardly, trying to see as little as possible. He was...oh yuck, thought Janey, he's cutting the whole head off. She closed her eyes. This was just great. She'd gone back to try to find a new doll for a girl and ended up watching some bloodthirsty guy cut the head off a deer. This was so disgusting!

"Hold her still!" Martin commanded. She opened her eyes slightly. He'd cut away all the skin and now he was...oh, gross...oh, man, he was slitting open the animal's stomach and now he was...

Janey let go and ran.

"Hey! You there! James! Come back here!" Martin stood up, his hands dripping red. "You bloody lazy fool! Get back here right now!"

Not a chance. Not all the tickets back to Toronto. Not having her mum come back from Turkey. No way was she going to turn around, she thought, as she plunged back onto the forested path where she'd left Mrs. Fisher and Louisa. They had to help her get out of here. Maybe Mrs. Fisher's magic could help.

There was no sign of the woman and child, but as she hurried through the woods, she caught sight of a man-made building at the end of the path. Coming closer, she realized she was facing a massive wall, almost as tall as the one that ran along the side of her two-storey school back in Toronto.

But this one was made of logs all stretching up to the darkening sky. How on earth did you get in?

She followed the wall around a corner, just as a small figure barrelled into her.

"Ooof. I've been watching for you," said Louisa, rubbing her forehead as she grinned up at Janey.

"Watching doesn't mean ramming me," grumbled Janey, rubbing her ribcage.

"What did you do with Martin?"

"I left him back there. I couldn't...I mean, I didn't..."

"It stinks, doesn't it?" said Louisa sympathetically. "I don't like the smell either." She grabbed Janey's hand, pulling her along the wall. "But you should've smelled the ice house this year. We had to move it, it stank so bad. Mama said that was because the men like Martin didn't want to climb down to the bottom to bring up the old meat and so it just started rotting."

She stopped to look up at Janey, her eyes alight. "Can you imagine? If you climb to the top of this wall and look down, that's how deep the pit in the icehouse is. And it's really, really dark in there. And to get to the meat at the bottom, you have to climb all the way down, with the awful smell, and the maggots and the drips from the ice melting..." She shivered deliciously, then started walking again. "I can't think about the ice house at night. It makes me feel too...too...tumbled in my stomach."

Janey made a mental note not to eat any meat at the fort.

They reached a huge gate, with a small, more human-sized door cut into it. Louisa pulled it open and slipped through. Janey followed.

In the light of the waning afternoon, a large, rectangular dirt courtyard surrounded on all sides by wooden buildings lay sprawled before them. Men in trousers and tunics, belted with long, bright red or blue sashes, ambled between the buildings.

"That's the Big House over there," said Louisa solemnly, nodding to a three-storey building across the yard. "Those windows there are called glass, but some of the Indians who come here think our Chief Factor, Mr. Rowand, has his own magic powers and can stop ice from melting in the summer."

"Too bad he couldn't use it in the ice house," said Janey.

Louisa giggled, but stopped abruptly as two figures, a Native man and a boy Janey's age, stepped from the building immediately on their left. The little girl drew herself up with as much dignity as a seven-year-old could muster. She stared resolutely away as the man and boy approached, arms laden with blankets. Janey and the boy exchanged curious glances, but not a word was said until the two walked past and out through the gate.

"That Black Bear. He thinks he's so clever," Louisa burst out as the door latched behind the pair. "Always boasting about how many furs he brings in. He says soon he'll hunt as many as his own father. Don't you think that's boastful? And he says hunting is so much better than trading. My father is a trader."

The Indian boy's name triggered something in Janey, but Louisa's voice – did that girl ever stop talking? – continued.

"But *he* can't speak English, and Father can speak English and French and Cree. I speak Cree too, because of Mama. And Father hunts when he travels to Fort Garry and York Factory. That's where he is right now – Fort Garry, I mean. He's looking for a home for us, he says. When his letter comes we'll..."

The wooden door burst open, interrupting the child. Scowling fiercely, Martin stepped through, with what looked like an oddly shaped crimson pillow draped over his shoulders. He slammed the door shut and continued forward until he saw Janey and Louisa.

"Well, if it isn't His Highness Good-for-Nothin' himself," snarled Martin, coming up close enough to just about touch Janey's nose with his. Overwhelmed by his bad breath, she realized too late what was slung about Martin's shoulders. Beheaded, skinned, and pathetically naked, a part of the deer's carcass was practically wrapped around Martin's ears. Janey stepped backward, trying not to gag.

"What – ya gonna run away on me again? Go get the other half, you lazy son of a..."

"Martin. I need the boy," a voice cut in from behind. "Give him what you've cut up so far, and he'll bring it to our quarters." Mrs. Fisher appeared in the shadows of a long, low building behind Janey. Disgusted, Martin flung the carcass on the ground at Janey's feet. "You hunted well, Martin," said Mrs. Fisher, before she disappeared into the building. Martin turned silently and left the fort.

"Come on then," said Louisa cheerfully. She bent down to grab the carcass around its ribs, but it was much too heavy for her. She looked up at Janey, who seemed riveted to the ground. "It doesn't smell so bad now. Really. And it will make fine meals for us. But I need your help."

Louisa was right. It hardly smelled at all, but it felt clammy and squishy. Janey swore that when she returned to her real life – whenever that happened – she would never again complain about bringing the groceries in from the car. Between them, the girls hauled the slippery carcass through the door Mrs. Fisher had entered and plopped it onto a wooden table.

The shadowy room was crowded with cupboards, chairs, and beds covered in Hudson's Bay Company blankets. Mrs. Fisher was by the fire, grilling squares of yellow bread over the flames. "Come here, boy." Lowering her voice, she looked up at Janey. "Why are you still here?"

"I don't know how to get back," said Janey, exasperated.

"Hush, boy. The other families." As her eyes grew accustomed to the dark, Janey realized that several youngsters were staring at her from behind one of the beds, while a woman nursed a baby in a dark corner.

"You live here? With others?" asked Janey. The room seemed small and cramped.

"The families of the traders live here, sharing work and space. It is a good place." Mrs. Fisher handed Janey and Louisa the toasted squares. "Come, I will walk with you to the Big House. Martha needs Louisa in the kitchen. You too."

"Cornbread!" said Louisa delightedly, skipping out the door. "Mama makes the best of all the..."

"Louisa, hush! I need to talk," said her mother sternly. She turned to Janey. "My magic cannot help you. If you cannot go back the way you have come, then perhaps your home is not where you think it is."

"Of course I know where my home is," snapped Janey. Granny's little white clapboard house and the brick duplex in Toronto sprang into her head at the same time. Confused, she continued, "Besides, I'm not here looking for a home; I'm supposed to stop a terrible thing."

"Yes," said Mrs. Fisher, sighing. They had reached the Big House. "Go with Louisa," she said finally. The child had already ducked through the door and down the stairs. Janey followed, entering the large, low-ceilinged kitchen dominated by a huge fireplace in its centre. A young woman chopping onions at the table greeted Louisa without even looking up.

"There you are, child. There's no time to waste. Factor Rowand is in a terrible fury. The York boats are late and nothing pleases him. Even his wife is annoyed and wants dinner immediately. Who's this now?" The woman had glanced up from her work.

"This is James, Martha. He's from Rocky Mountain House. I think he's waiting for the boats too. But he's here to help," said Louisa, grabbing a knife and heading toward the potatoes.

Janey followed, but Martha stopped her. "First the firewood. You'll find some out back. And don't dawdle."

Janey stumbled back out into the evening, and waited for her eyes to adjust. True enough, a pile of wood crouched by the wall. She grabbed an armful of short logs and turned, then stopped. A figure barred her way.

"Well, at least ya can manage to pick up a few sticks of wood without runnin' away," sneered Martin from the darkness. "Hangin' round with the womenfolk in the kitchens to avoid doin' any real work, are ya?"

Janey tried to make her way around Martin, but his arm shot out and grabbed the sleeve of her shirt. The firewood tumbled from her hands. "Can't even do that, can ya?" said Martin, drawing her close enough that she could smell his dinner on his breath. She sensed, more than saw, that his other arm was swinging toward her. Instinctively, Janey ducked, grabbing one of the dropped sticks of wood. She whacked it at him, then reached down to grab another.

"Jamie, if you don't bring the wood soon, Martha said she'll come out here and thrash anyone keeping her from putting dinner on the table." Louisa's little figure stood backlit at the door.

Martin stepped back, his hand clutching the side of his face. "We're not done yet," he hissed, turning into the darkness.

Shaking, Janey scooped up the wood she'd dropped and returned to the kitchen. The next hour hardly gave her a chance to think as she hauled water, fetched supplies, and scrubbed pots under Martha's stern eye. When the dinner had been served, the cook stepped out from the heat of the kitchen, leaving Janey and Louisa to start with the dishes. The odd slide-pound, slide-pound noise that Janey had heard intermittently started up again overhead. "What *is* that sound?"

"That's Chief Factor Rowand," said Louisa. "Black Bear's people call him 'Big Mountain,' but the men in the fort call him One-Pound-One – only, never in front of him. Years and years ago he went hunting and he fell off his horse and hurt his leg. Ever since, when he walks around, he makes that noise."

She dried another plate, listening to the steps above, then giggled. "Mama says that on the day of the accident, her friend Lisette was working here at the fort. Mr. Rowand didn't come back and didn't come back, so she took a wagon out to find him. And then, when she did, Lisette wouldn't bring him back until he said he'd marry her. That's how come she's the most powerful woman here."

Louisa put the plates in the cupboard. "Mama says a girl ought to tell her man what she wants *before* she marries. That way, there aren't any surprises." They listened again as the odd footsteps thumped overhead.

"He must be worried," Louisa continued. "But so is Mama. And I want the boats to come too. Then we'll finally have news of Father. We've been waiting for his letter since he left last spring."

"Why's he gone so long?" asked Janey, carefully washing knives.

"For many years he has worked for the Hudson's Bay Company and now he wants his own home. He's looking for a home for us in Fort Garry. As soon as his letter comes, Mama and I will leave. Father says there are houses – regular houses – and streets in Fort Garry. I've never seen a street. Here there's just the fort, the river, and the woods."

Martha swept back in just as the last dish was cleared away. "Well now, we might have a bite of something before I send you back." She sliced several pieces from a leftover roast, as well as two thick slabs of heavy dark bread.

"Go on now. Bring it over to the fire and we can have a chat."

Tales of the icehouse fresh in her mind, Janey opted for a plain slice of bread. As she pulled a chair to the fire, Martha eyed her expectantly.

"So. Tell us what's new at Rocky Mountain House," she said encouragingly.

Panicking, Janey glanced at Louisa, who was dragging a chair up beside her. "Martha, please, please tell the story about Mama and the ghost," Louisa begged. "I told about how Mama was magic but not how it started. And you tell it the best."

Flattered, Martha forgot her own request. "Well, let's see now. It was before my time, but my mama was there when it happened." She settled herself into her chair.

"A long time ago," she began, "back when there were two trading companies here, Louisa's grandfather, Mr. King, worked for the North West Company just down here on the river, at Fort Augustus.

"Now, one day, in the middle of winter, Mr. King was preparing to leave on a three-day trading trip. But another man, called La Mothe, he heard about these Indians too, and he wanted to trade with them for his own company.

"The night before Mr. King left, the master of the Hudson's Bay Company came to him." Martha's voice deepened. "'Be careful, Mr. King. That man La Mothe has a terrible temper and has been known to shoot people who get in his way.'

"But Mr. King just laughed and said, 'To be shot by La Mothe...that would be a good joke indeed!' Mr. King didn't believe anything could hurt him, but his wife was worried and begged him not to go.

"Still, he spent the night as usual in the tent with his small family; his wife and his little daughter, Marie, who is Louisa's mama, and who was even smaller than our Louisa here. Next morning he set out in his sleigh, still chuckling over his wife's fears.

"But two nights later, when all were fast asleep and the only sound was the fire crackling inside the warm tent, Mrs. King woke up. Little Marie was weeping.

"'Mother,' she cried, pointing to an empty space in front of her, 'there is Father at the foot of the bed and, oh, how terrible. Look! His neck is all red.'" Martha aimed her finger at the fire, while Louisa unconsciously put her hand up to her throat.

"Mrs. King hushed Marie. 'It is only a bad dream, little one. You must go back to sleep.' Marie finally stopped crying and curled up in her nest of winter furs, as did her mother.

"But hardly an hour passed before she woke once more. Little Marie was weeping and cried out again: 'There is Father at the foot of the bed. Oh, look, look! His neck is all red.' Once again Mrs. King hushed her little girl and put her back to sleep.

"But now, while Marie slept, Mrs. King tossed and turned in the furs, worrying, worrying. Finally, in the morning, she told some others what her daughter had seen the night before. They laughed, and told her that Marie was just a little girl with funny dreams. Almost everyone forgot the story...until the next afternoon.

"Watchmen saw the sleigh from the bastion of the fort and opened the main gate. In flew the horses, shaking and whinnying, eyes big with fright. They couldn't see Mr. King anywhere. But when they finally calmed the horses and looked in the bottom of the sleigh, there he was, dead. La Mothe had shot him through the throat and the frozen blood crusted red against his neck.

"To this day, Marie – well, Mrs. Fisher – says the ghost of her father came back to her the night he died, to say goodbye to his daughter."

In the silence that followed, the darkness outside the ring of firelight felt gloomy and menacing. Little wonder all three jumped when the kitchen door banged open and Martin burst in. "The York boats are comin'. We need all hands to unload." He glanced meaningfully at Janey, who caught sight of a thin trickle of blood on his right cheek before he clattered down the corridor.

It was only when Janey stepped outside into the court-yard that she suddenly grasped how dark it had become. Flickers from candles and hearth fires shimmered through small windows, but all else was black.

Not quite. Janey glanced up and caught her breath. Never before had she seen so many stars glitter so fiercely. There were millions of them, whole dazzling blankets tossed carelessly above her. She resisted the impulse to reach up, to touch them as they sparkled so close. Janey gave her head a shake. The girls back home would think she'd lost her mind. It must be some weird optical illusion, she figured, like those 3-D glasses they gave you for certain movies.

She glanced back down again, and her eyes, adjusted to the dark, made out the circle of log buildings around her. It occurred to her that she might have to spend the night here in this place of woodsmoke and dead animals, with no way home. What had she done? And why, oh why, was she here? Beyond the thin wooden walls of the fort were woods and prairie and...nothing else, in a massive expanse of wilderness. She was merely a tiny little creature who couldn't even begin to stop anything bad from happening. The darkness crowded in on her, making Janey feel cold and small and frightened.

"Are ya prayin' or just hidin' from the work again?" sneered a voice in her ear. She recognized Martin's stinky breath – someone should give that guy a toothbrush – and stumbled after Louisa, who was waiting impatiently by the gate.

Down at the river's edge, men were slapping each other on the back, while others were already unloading packages from the boat. A mixture of French and English shouts and curses wove through the air, blending with the smell of sweat and woodsmoke. Hands pushed Janey forward, and before she knew it, she was standing waist deep in water, grasping a huge round object with a pleasantly sweet smell to it.

"Ya gonna smoke that tobacco right where yer standin', lad, or are ya gonna take it to shore?" asked a man from the flat, shallow-bottomed boat.

"That one's too lazy to do anything," said Martin, lumbering up. In the moonlight she could see a long cut that ran from his eye down across his cheekbone. She stepped quickly away, clutching the tobacco cake to her. She dropped it on a pile at the shore, where Louisa, her mother, and some other women stood waiting.

"Has the post been unloaded?" asked Louisa eagerly. Even Mrs. Fisher was looking on with interest.

"I'll ask." Janey waded back in and repeated the question.

"Here ya go, lad," said the fellow, tossing her a leather bag. Just as she was about to grab it, a sharp kick slammed into the side of her knee, sending Janey toppling into the water. The bag landed with a sickening splash in the river. Finding her feet, she reached desperately for several papers floating off in the current.

"Ya stupid oaf! Can't ya do anythin'? Don't ya know how important the post is to the people here?" Martin fished the bag from the water and handed it to one of the men going by. "Yer just a lazy, stupid, good-for-nothin' oaf, causin' trouble," he said, advancing on Janey and giving her a mighty push backwards.

Janey went under, then sputtered back up, panicking, and tried to get around Martin. But he shoved her again, driving her deeper into the river. She resurfaced and looked for help, but the crowd had gathered around the leather bag on the shore. Martin plunged at her once more, this time hanging onto her as he pushed her under water. Terrified, Janey drew up her knee and kicked him, hard. He let go, and Janey burst to the surface, gasping for breath and paddling backwards out of his reach.

"Why, ya little..." Martin lunged forward, and Janey flipped onto her stomach and swam for all she was worth, ignoring the pull of her bulky clothes. She could hear the splashing behind her as Martin cursed and swore. Janey swam steadily forward, hoping he'd never learned to swim. Now men were running along the shore, calling and shouting. When she reached the opposite side, she pulled herself out of the water. Cold, wet, frightened, she scanned the riverbank for a path into the bush, then froze. The moon's reflection caught in a pair of eyes staring at her from the underbrush.

Terrified, Janey turned the other way and plunged into the trees. Ahead, she saw a path and dashed toward it. Something was following and Janey tried to put as much distance between her and those eyes as she could.

But she was tiring, and the path, with its turns and twists, was climbing uphill. Frantically, she stared up the trail, looking for a place to hide. She could still hear shouts from the river, and footfalls behind her. Should she climb a tree? Turn and face her pursuer? The stitch in her side was becoming unbearable. Just as she thought she could not take another step, she saw it – a rock overhang, and underneath, an opening, dark and still. A branch snapped somewhere behind her, propelling Janey toward the hole. She stuck her feet in first, praying it wasn't an animal hole, and turned to confront her follower.

Two things came to her at the same time as she slid down. One was that the hole had no bottom. The second was that her pursuer was that Indian boy, Black Bear.

CHAPTER FIVE

THE FUR TRADERS MUST HAVE FOUND HER, THOUGHT
Janey, opening her eyes. She blinked. It was bright
day. But the two men coming toward her were
dressed in hard hats and clutching modern-looking walkie-
talkies. She sat up and grabbed the locket, which was sliding
off her lap.

"Hey, you! Whaddya doin' in here? Can't you read? It's
way too dangerous for you to be here," called one of the
men. No kidding, thought Janey as she scrambled to her
feet, brushed off the dirt, and edged toward where she'd
stashed her backpack.

"Sorry. I, uh, I dropped something. My grandmother's
locket," said Janey, holding the silver necklace up as proof.

"It doesn't matter if it's the crown jewels. You're not supposed to be in a construction site," said the second man as
they came up to her. "Man, what happened to you?"

He'd never, ever, believe it, she thought, glancing down at her muddy, steaming overalls. "Look, I'm sorry. I'll try not to let it happen again," she said. She vaulted over the fence, swooped up her pack, and ran.

"Hey! We're not done with you yet! Come back here!"

You gotta be kidding, thought Janey, plunging into an ice cream parlour directly ahead of her. A family with three kids, clustered around the display case, looked up, startled, as she rushed past. She smiled weakly at them, and kept going toward the back of the shop, where a door was propped open to let in the summer breeze.

Once outside, she slowed and looked around. The sunlight was fierce and dazzling after the darkness at the fort. I need a plan, thought Janey, panting. I need to stop running. I need to...I really need to get out of these clothes.

To her right she noticed a two-storey white building with a back entrance. Janey slipped through the door and found a women's washroom. She hardly recognized the figure staring back at her in the mirror over the sink. Every last bit of her face was covered with smoke and grime that not even her river swim had washed away. Her overalls were a mess and her sneakers... How was she supposed to explain this to Granny?

She stripped off the shirt and overalls and, as she was stuffing them into her backpack, she noticed a twenty-dollar bill in one of the pockets. Well, at least I've found the money I thought I'd lost, she thought. Maybe it just doesn't work in olden-days time, like my watch.

She straightened and inspected herself. At least her shorts

and T-shirt had stayed pretty clean, though they were still damp. Janey figured they'd dry in the sun. She grabbed a handful of paper towels and worked on her face. She smiled, remembering Louisa's comment about her fish-belly white skin, then stopped. The memory of the little girl waiting eagerly on the riverbank for word from her father flooded back. Because of Janey, there would be no word.

Scrubbing fiercely at a black streak on her forehead, she tried to ignore the rush of confusion and guilt threatening to sweep down on her. What was she doing here, falling down tunnels, fighting with fur traders, losing important letters that could change a child's life? And why had she even bothered to come back, when it seemed as if all she did was get herself and people she liked into serious trouble? Anna's tent and her doll flashed through Janey's mind, then the letters, white in the moonlight, smudges of blue ink weeping off the page. Janey felt her eyes begin to prickle with tears.

And what about Martin? He probably couldn't even swim. What if she'd drowned him? Even though he was crazy, she didn't want to be responsible for his death.

That's it, she vowed. I'm never going to meddle in the past again. Who am I kidding? I can't stop something terrible from happening. What a stupid idea. Stupid park. Stupid mother for taking a stupid job in stupid Turkey. Stupid old woman for telling me about this stupid "bad thing" in the first place. Janey flung the paper towels into the garbage angrily, and walked out.

The sun was warm on her face, and in the gentle heat of the summer afternoon, Janey felt the tension seep out of her body. It was a gorgeous day, and people were ambling past in shorts and sandals, taking in the sights. You know, thought Janey, I really ought to try and have a look around here without leaping into open pits. Maybe I could find out what I need to know. Maybe I don't even have to go back. It could all be right around here.

She stepped into the path of a costumed woman in a long skirt and oversized hat walking toward her. Two girls, in aproned dresses and straw boaters, trailed after her.

"Excuse me. Is there some kind of a fort, or an Edmonton House, around here?"

The woman nodded. "It's at the end, or at the very beginning, of this park, depending on how you look at it," said the woman, smiling.

"Mother, just tell her where it is," said the older girl, rolling her eyes.

"Well, you could turn right at 1885 Street and then follow its curve to the fort, or you could take the shortcut..."

Janey interrupted the woman. "What do you mean, 1885 Street?"

"Well, there are four different time periods in this park. We're on 1905 Street, and there's 1885 Street, and the fort era..." Four time periods, thought Janey. Maybe that's where she'd gone wrong! She had just drifted into the wrong era when she tried to get back to Anna. And maybe she wasn't even supposed to meet Anna. Maybe the terrible thing she was supposed to stop was...whoa. Hold on here. Hadn't she just told herself she was going to stay out of trouble? But what if she'd just taken a wrong turn in the tunnels? Maybe if...

"Is there anything else we can help you with?" asked the woman in the large hat. The two girls were staring at her, puzzled.

"Um, yeah." Janey shook herself. "That shortcut?"

"Just follow the streetcar tracks, then cut through on your right. You can't miss it," said the older girl. "Tall, wooden walls..."

"About two storeys high? Yeah, I think I've got it." As Janey moved away from them, she pictured the tall fort, and the boy Black Bear leaving through the gate with his father. That same niggling feeling poked at her again when she thought about the boy's name. Where had she heard it before? She mentally scrambled through the events of the past few days, searching, and then it came to her. Black Bear had the same name as that old woman she'd met with Anna!

Janey looked up from the edge of the sidewalk in excitement, then froze, and felt the hair on her arms tingling. The wooden house and that barn; she'd seen them before. The round barn was the same one she'd seen when she'd met up with Mrs. Henderson. It was a little closer to the house maybe, but the same size, the same height. This is just so creepy, thought Janey. I've never been here before, but I have. Am I awake? Am I dreaming? Am I here?

When the screen door burst open, Janey just about jumped out of her skin. But this was a very different Mrs. Henderson, who probably didn't have a pair of itchy woollen stockings hidden somewhere in the kitchen. Janey backed away quietly and turned in the direction of the fort.

The walls, when she reached them, were as high as she

remembered. She glanced around, half expecting a little girl with Louisa's sparkling eyes to come barrelling around the corner. Grow up, Janey, she said to herself. A train whistle pierced her thoughts and a conductor called out, "Last train back to the station." Janey glanced at her watch, and realized that if she didn't hurry back, Granny would be kept waiting. She made her way to the platform and climbed on board.

THERE WAS NO YELLOW CADILLAC idling anywhere when Janey went through the exit. She poked her way through the parking lot, looking for a telltale gleam of chrome somewhere between the trucks and vans baking in the afternoon sun.

"Hey, Janey!" The call came from a small blue hatchback one row over. Mike was standing by the back door, waving wildly. The girl from this morning – what was her name? – was sitting in front with the window rolled down, picking at her fingernails with a bored expression. Great, just what I need, thought Janey, trudging over.

"You're supposed to come home with us. Your Grandma sent us over to get you," said Mike when Janey got closer. He scooted over to the far seat, leaving the door open for her. Before Janey could hesitate, the woman in the driver's seat leaned across the girl and said, "Hi, Janey. I'm Jo Wegner, Mike and Nicky's mum. Your grandmother was just feeling a little tired and I offered to pick you up. Besides, these guys were turning into baked prunes down at the pool."

The girl in the front seat rolled her eyes. "We were NOT, Mother."

"That's because you hardly stuck your big toe in the water," said Mike. "You were too busy ogling that one lifeguard."

"Not a chance! He's not my type. Too much brawn, too little brain. Besides, you were so busy doing cannonballs with Ben and Graeme and Ryan that there was hardly any water in the pool."

"That's because you and your friends climbed out and the water levels dropped by..."

"Guys! Enough!" Mrs. Wegner turned to Janey. "Can you guess that they're twins?"

Janey climbed in and shut the door, wondering what was wrong with Granny. She tried shoving her grubby runners under the seat in front of her, but Mike seemed not to notice.

"So you wanna come with me an' Nicky to the pool tomorrow?" asked Mike.

"Gee, Mike, you sound like a talking Sammy," said Nicky from the front seat. "'Ya wanna come, huh? Huh? Pant! Pant!' Maybe she's got better things to do. Maybe she's more interested in *history*," Nicky made it sound like a dirty word, "than hanging out at a swimming pool with us."

Janey felt the blood rush up to her cheeks. It wasn't the history that had drawn her here, she thought. It was Anna's doll and her feeling of guilt.

"Nicky, Mike was just trying to be friendly," said Mrs. Wegner. "And it can't be easy for Janey out here all alone with just her grandmother for company."

Despite the open windows, silence smothered the inside of the car. Janey peeked at Mike, who was staring resolutely out his side. Then she caught Mrs. Wegner's eye in the rear-view mirror.

"So, what grade are you going into, Janey?"

Oh, no. Now I'm going to get the standard adult grilling, thought Janey. Do they take a course in this before they turn twenty-one? "Seven," said Janey dutifully. If she asks me what my favourite subjects are, I'll scream.

"That's just like Mike and Nicky. So what are your favourite subjects? Our Nicky is the drama queen of the family, and Mike can do math problems that can cross my eyes."

Okay, I won't scream. But if she asks me what I wanna be when I grow up, I'm going to get out of the car. "Language Arts, I guess."

"I always liked English when I was at school. You must like reading. What books are you reading these days? I wonder if..."

"Oh, Mother, puh-lease. It's like you're interviewing her for a job or something. Stop grilling her," sniped Nicky. "Besides, it's all pretty obvious. Let me guess," she continued, putting a hand to her forehead as if she was communing with some faraway spirit. "She's twelve, she's going into junior high, she's read *Anne of Green Gables,* she thinks Edmonton is incredibly boring, and she'd much rather be back in Toronto with all her cool friends."

Man. What's up with her? thought Janey. Just because I miss my friends doesn't mean she has to... The car turned onto Granny's street and Janey had to grip the armrest to keep from leaning into Mike. At least she doesn't have a sick grandmother weighing her down. I'll show her, she thought, righting herself. "I'd love to come with you tomorrow," she said, her eyes challenging Nicky in the rear-view mirror.

"Great," said Mike. "We usually head over around eleven. And bring along something to eat, otherwise you have to go home during the best part of the day."

"Bye, Janey. Tell your grandmother that if she needs anything else, she should just call," Mrs. Wegner said as Janey stepped from the car.

The house was cool and dark inside. "Janey?" The blinds in Granny's bedroom were pulled down firmly against the light. She looked thin and gaunt lying on the bed, the bones of her face making funny shadows as Janey looked down at her.

"You all right, Granny?"

"I'm fine, kiddo, just a little tired. I'm sorry I couldn't pick you up."

"It's okay. I'm going to the pool with them tomorrow."

"Oh, good. Did you have fun at the park? You know, I forgot to tell you that your great-grandfather worked for the Hudson's Bay Company."

"At a fort like the one in the park?" A shiver of excitement crept through Janey. Maybe this was the clue! Maybe this was why she'd been sent back.

"Oh, no, dear, nothing as grand as all that. It was just a small outpost in northern Alberta, as near as I can remember. I was quite young. We left there shortly after your great-grandfather died."

Another dead end. "Did you move to this house?"

"Oh no. We lived downtown all through the war. It was

only after I married your grandfather that we moved here. He was very proud of this little house. And I've lived here ever since."

Janey looked at the walls of the darkened bedroom and imagined living in one place for decades and decades. Somehow it seemed impossible. Her own parents had moved at least three times that she could remember. Dimly she recalled a house with a huge yard and a playset from when she was little. The next house was smaller, and now their home was about the same size as Granny's, if you counted her basement. At least it wasn't a tent, or one dark room shared with another family.

"Would you mind just fixing something for yourself tonight, dear? I think the weather's just too hot for me to eat."

"Sure, Granny, I'm happy with a peanut butter sandwich." The shadows playing across her grandmother's face looked soft and gentle. "What'll we do tonight? Watch a little TV, or will you show me how to cheat at rummy?"

The shadows disappeared when Granny grinned. "Let's start with some TV and see if you're up to it before the news comes on."

THE NIGHTS AND DAYS slipped into a comfortable routine. Janey didn't mind. After the excitement of two trips to Fort Edmonton Park, she just wanted normal. Weeks passed, mostly down at the pool, hanging out with Mike and, eventually, Nicky. Remembering the nasty business with Martin, Janey didn't want to get on anyone's bad side. She finally figured out that Nicky thought Janey was just a stuck-up kid from Toronto who didn't like anything about Edmonton.

Things changed on a particularly gloomy and overcast morning when Mrs. Wegner offered to take her and the twins to West Edmonton Mall. Janey's wild enthusiasm for the waterslides and roller coaster rides seemed to reassure Nicky. And when Janey told her that the rides at Klondike Days were the same ones she rode at the Canadian National Exhibition, Nicky figured that the girl from the East might not be so bad. The next day she showed Janey how to e-mail her friends from the public library.

Having access to e-mail meant Janey could keep in touch with her friends without pestering Granny about long-distance calls. She dashed messages off to Rebecca, Kira, and the others immediately, and then waited. And waited.

They're probably off doing some really cool stuff, thought Janey, who had ridden Granny's old one-speed to the library three days running without findng any replies. When she finally got one from Kira on the fourth day, it was disappointingly short.

"Hi Jane-o! Thanx for your message. It's hot here. We're just hangin' out at the park. Gotta go. Me an' Rachel are going to buy Slurps. She says HI." The one from Deanna was hardly better.

Aaargh! What kind of a message is that? I practically beg them for news, and no one sends me anything except lame notes and stupid forwards. She smashed down on the keyboard, and a librarian looked at her disapprovingly.

Yeah, yeah, I'm going, she thought, logging off. She

pushed through the doors of the brick building and un-chained the bike.

In fairness, though, it's not as if I was writing them a lot of interesting stuff, thought Janey. I mean, I can't even begin to e-mail them about crashing into two different historical time zones. They wouldn't believe me.

As the weeks went by, Janey was even beginning to doubt her own memories. She'd gone back into the garage once, to study the button she'd tucked into the overall pockets before she'd packed them away with the shirt and cap. But what did the button tell her? Not much, except she had a loose button that could, really, have come from anywhere. Exasperated, Janey slammed the trunk lid down and a whiff of woodsmoke rose up around her.

The fact that there were four different eras at the park nagged at Janey. Her mind kept returning to the cave she'd landed in after she jumped into the construction pit, and the more she thought about it, the more it seemed to her that one tunnel was missing that second time. She'd only had three ways to choose from, and the first time, she was sure, she'd had four.

If the four tunnels represented the four different eras at the park, maybe she just hadn't picked the right era to visit. What if she went back again and there were only two tunnels now? She'd have fifty-fifty odds of picking the right one, and then she'd be able to do what she was supposed to, what that Mrs. Black Bear had told her.

Janey stood up abruptly from where she'd been sitting on the trunk. No way. Nope. It just wasn't worth it. She was having a nice enough little summer here. She'd just hang on until the end of August, then she'd go home and meet up with her old friends again and start junior high and life would be perfect.

"Janey?" Granny stood in the doorway, her slight frame outlined by the afternoon sun. "I know it's a lot to ask, but I was wondering if you'd come with me to my appointment. I'd just like...your company."

Janey came up to Granny. "What's this appointment for?" The force of her question seemed to make Granny take a step back.

"It's just a checkup, kiddo, nothing serious. I probably shouldn't even have asked... It's just that it's so...so gloomy in a hospital."

Janey put her arm gently on her grandmother's shoulders. "Course I'll come, Granny. And after, how about I treat you to a Slurpee?"

LATE, LATE THAT NIGHT, so late, in fact, that it was already early in the morning, Janey dreamed that a group of angry fur traders waving wet letters in the air were blocking fire trucks from reaching Anna's burning tent. The fire trucks kept ringing and ringing, but the fur traders refused to move. Granny stood on the other side of the trucks, calling her. "Janey! Janey! Hey, kiddo!" Though Janey knew, somehow, that this was a dream, she was still furious because she couldn't get close to Granny. Someone shook her shoulders, and Janey woke.

"Janey! It's your mum. She's on the phone, all the way

from Turkey." In the early morning light, Janey stared blankly at Granny, whose fragile skull gleamed through the tufts of hair sprouting on her head.

"The telephone, kiddo. In the kitchen."

Janey stumbled out of the bedroom and reached for the receiver. "Mummy?!"

"Hi, sweetie. I'm sorry I woke you. But I just had a sudden yearning to hear my baby's voice. How are you doing?"

"I'm all right."

"Are you keeping busy? Tell me what you're doing."

Janey yawned. It was awfully early. "I go down to that pool Daddy always talked about, even on days when it's not so warm. Granny lets me use her bike. I've been to the mall; the big one. I guess you know that part. Did you get my e-mail?"

"I did. I'm glad you've found a way to get on-line. Still, every so often I just need to hear my girl talk to me."

"Are you okay? How's your project coming along?"

"It's going really well. Everyone here seems to be quite excited about it. In fact, they've asked me to do more work for them after this."

"Does this mean you're not coming home at the end of the summer?"

"No-o-o," said Janey's mum, slowly. "I'll be back, but I'll be leaving again. I've even had a phone call from someone in Mexico."

"Mexico! That's, like, a whole continent away! Are you just abandoning me and Daddy here in Canada?"

"No, darling, of course not. Just because I'm away from

you doesn't mean I don't miss you guys desperately. In fact, if the next project goes ahead, I was kind of hoping you might fly out with me for a week or two."

"To Turkey? That would be so cool!" Janey was now wide awake.

"Now, don't start packing suitcases yet. We're still dealing with the paperwork, and that always takes forever. What's going on there? Is Granny doing better? She said you were being a big help to her. Are you really doing some gardening for her?"

"Yeah, well, it's not that hard. You throw in a few seeds, stomp down the dirt, turn on the sprinkler. The sunflowers are already up to my knees. We might have to dig up the concrete in our backyard when I get back to Toronto."

"I don't think the landlord's going to like that." Her mother's chuckle made Janey's heart lurch.

"I miss you, Mum. It's okay here, and I even have some friends, but I really want to have you around."

"Darling, it won't be too long now. Have you heard from Dad yet?"

"Why? Is he coming out? When? Soon?"

"Oh dear, I hope I haven't let the cat out of the bag and this was supposed to be a surprise. Look, I've got to go; my taxi's here. I'm supposed to be having dinner at some swanky hotel with the mucky-mucks who make all the decisions."

"Wait! Mummy! There's so much more I need to..." Janey's sleep-sloshed mind was struggling to tell...what? Her mum waited quietly on the line.

"Good luck with your meeting, Mummy. Love you."

"Love you forever, darling." Janey listened for the dial tone before she hung up the phone. Then she turned to her grandmother.

"Granny! Is Daddy supposed to be coming out here?"

Granny's eyes twinkled. "Was I meant to tell you that? I thought it was a surprise. Did I get it wrong?"

"Granny! Tell me! Please, please, please!?!"

"And ruin the surprise?"

"Then he *is* coming out! Don't look so innocent, Granny. I know you know something. So. When's he coming?"

"Well, I'm not sure if your mother got mixed up with the time change and thought he was coming last night..."

"Last night!?"

"...but he's arriving today at noon."

At the airport Granny took a seat close to the exit doors. "You go ahead, kiddo, and bring him here. It'll spoil him to have too many females drooling over him."

Janey stood at the foot of the escalator, barely able to keep from jumping up and down. She had a sudden craving for one of her dad's famous, feet-off-the-floor, twirl-in-the-air bear hugs. It occurred to her that she and Granny hadn't had a good squeeze since the last time they'd been at the airport. And that was probably because Janey was afraid of hurting her, so fragile did her grandmother seem these days.

"Hi, sweetheart." Her dad stood before her, looking down at her with the familiar crinkly lines radiating from his eyes. Janey flung her arms around his neck and instantly her feet were in the air and she was spinning around the arrival lounge, whooping in delight. Finally, he set her back down.

"I think I just smashed your feet against that poor woman's bag," said her dad, panting and grinning down at her. "Where's Granny?"

"Hello, Alex," said Granny, coming forward.

Turning, her dad dropped his arms from Janey's side and paused a moment. Then he folded his mother gently in his arms. No wild bear hugs for her.

IT TOOK THREE DAYS for Janey to find out why her dad had really come to Edmonton. They'd had a great time until then. He took his "two girls," as he called them, out for dinner twice, and told Janey all the news of her friends, gleaned from two chance meetings with Becca and Rachel at the video store. He admired Janey's work in Granny's garden and walked the neighbourhood with her, showing her some of his favourite childhood hangouts.

It was on one of those walks through the ravine – after a liberal dose of bug repellent – that her dad told her what had happened.

"In a nutshell, Janey, I've been laid off," he said as they stopped on a wooden footbridge to watch the creek trickle by underneath.

"Laid off? They fired you?"

"No, not fired. I didn't do anything wrong. But there's no more work for me. It's just a bad time in the computer industry and has been for the past year."

"But what about those people in Seattle?"

"It fell through, Janey. In fact, I was hoping the Seattle stuff would lead to a new job. It's been looking bad for a while. It was really lucky Mummy got that assignment in Turkey."

"You mean she wasn't just going to Turkey because she thought it would be cool?"

"Well, she thought it would be cool, but she certainly didn't want to leave us – you – for such a long period. But things, as I said, were already looking shaky this spring."

Panic suddenly gripped Janey. "There's nothing shaky between the two of you, is there? Are you guys...are you two...still married?"

Janey's dad laughed ruefully as he pulled her close to him. "Of course we are, sweetheart. We love each other as much as we did on the day we were married, probably more."

They both leaned against the railing, watching the creek. "So what happens when you're unemployed?" Janey asked finally.

"Well, Mummy's job means we don't have to do anything drastic yet. But sitting around in Toronto twiddling my thumbs while you're out here doesn't really appeal to me." He paused, watching a twig float past. "So I was kinda thinking that maybe I'd move back here, with you."

Janey stared at him. "What do you mean, move? Like, for the rest of the summer?"

"Well, probably for longer than that, until the economy picks up. We could save some money..."

"You're crazy!" Janey pulled away from him. "Leave everyone and everything that I know and love, to move here?" Janey's voice rose until she was shouting. "That's the worst idea you've ever come up with! No wonder they fired you! Move away from all my friends in Toronto, from school, from...from...everything? Move here?! No way! You're just –"

"Janey! Whoa! Hold on here –"

"No! This is stupid! I'm not listening to this..." Furious, Janey turned and flew up the path, leaving her father far behind. How can he possibly think I'd want to move here? she thought. What a stupid, stupid idea. Why did he have to go and lose his job? And why did they need to move? Other people lost their jobs and they stayed at the same place. They went to the same school and...and...nothing changed. Everything was moving so fast here.

She reached her grandmother's garage and stood panting beside it. No way was she going to let anyone talk her into moving. This was just such a disaster. This was worse than...than losing some dumb letters in a river. This was a catastrophe. This was...this had to be stopped.

Janey's heart skipped a beat. If ever there was a disaster she was meant to stop, this was it! This was what she was supposed to be doing when she went into the past! Somehow she was linked to Edmonton's history, and if she could just get to the right point, she could convince her dad that he didn't need to move back here – that it would be okay to stay in Toronto. Somehow, she was the connection, because otherwise some other kid would be crawling through those tunnels. Janey fingered the locket around her neck and made a decision.

Five minutes later she was wheeling Granny's bike from the garage, clad in the coveralls and flannel shirt. The cap was stuck in her pocket. It took a half-hour of riding to get her to the park. She paid her admission and strode directly to the construction site, removing the locket from around her neck as she walked. When she reached the fence, she leaped over and dropped the locket to the ground. She was swallowed instantly.

CHAPTER SIX

WHAT WOULD IT TAKE TO REMEMBER TO BRING A flashlight? grumbled Janey, pulling herself out of the dirt and sitting up in the darkness. She fumbled for her watch and pushed the button for the light.

She'd been right. Now there were only two corridors leading away. Janey released her watch and saw, once again, a faint glimmer of light down the tunnel on her left. Nothing but darkness on the right.

Considering all the awful things that had happened when Janey had chosen the last two tunnels, maybe, she thought, she should go down the path that was dark. She went so far as to stick her head into the opening, then panicked. It was too black, too spooky. She pulled back and turned toward the opening on her left.

As she crawled along, Mrs. Black Bear's words about dressing warmly rushed back toward her. The closer she came to the surface, the colder the earth became. At the mouth of the tunnel, Janey realized she could see her breath in the sunlight. It was going to be cold here, and all she was wearing was a flannel shirt and overalls on top of summer clothes. She thought longingly of the coat in her grandfather's trunk.

Pulling herself cautiously from her hole, Janey scanned her surroundings for possible dangers. Before her, the river was clogged with huge chunks of ice. Dirty patches of snow and piles of soggy, dead leaves mottled the ground. The few trees that clung to the riverbank were naked and scraggly, though Janey noticed hints of green buds forming on the tips of the branches. And the sun was making an attempt to melt the snow, thought Janey grimly. As far as she could see, there were no other people about.

Yet as she clambered to her feet, Janey became aware of a steady hammering. Even a city girl like her knew that this wasn't some odd woodpecker burrowing into bark, but the sound of someone building something. She stepped gingerly around the snow patches and followed the noise up the side of the embankment. By the time she'd reached a stand of fir trees at the top and hidden herself behind them, the steady hammering had stopped, replaced by the sound of angry voices.

In a clearing before her stood the skeleton of a small house, its freshly cut wooden frame as bare and sparse as the poplars in the background. Inside the house frame, a small canvas tent flapped noisily whenever a chilly gust of wind caught its opening. But the sound wasn't enough to drown out the half-dozen men crowding threateningly around the unfinished doorway.

"Now look here, George. Be reasonable," said one voice from the back of the crowd. "You have no right to be settlin' on this land. You're jumpin' this claim, and if everyone starts doin' that we won't have any kinda order out here."

"You tell 'im, Wilson!" called another man. "If we let this one go, then no man can turn his back on his claim for an instant without losin' it." Grumbles and mutterings rose from the rest of the group.

"I'm tellin' you again," said a hoarse voice from just inside the door frame. "There's never been anyone on this particular land to develop it, and I have just as much right as anybody to settle it."

"You ain't got the right, George. This land was divided up fair and square after the men left the fort and it ain't yours to jump."

"Pa?" A small boy scooted through the wooden frame. "Why are these men shoutin' at you?"

"Because they haven't heard that on the Lord's Day a body shouldn't raise his voice in anger," said the hoarse voice, gentler now.

"You still oughtn't to be here, George." The grumblings died down. "Let's leave off for today, men. But be warned, George. If you're still here tomorrow, we're goin' to get you off this land, whatever it takes." Muttering amongst themselves, the men drifted toward their horses and slowly rode away.

The man left standing in the doorway eyed the

retreating group warily. "Son, I want you to follow them and see what they're plannin'. Take some of that bread and bacon with you, and find out what they're sayin' at the smithy's or McDougall's store."

The child ducked into the tent, emerging several minutes later, fists stuffed with provisions. His father smiled briefly.

"You're only goin' into town, Lucas, not clear across the territory. Best have some of that now, and put the rest in your pocket." The boy nodded, crammed half a fist into his mouth, and then headed in the direction of the men. Janey edged around the clearing and followed, as the sound of slow and steady hammering rang out behind her.

But the noise did little to muffle Janey's movements, and the sparse winter woods offered nothing in the way of camouflage. The small boy turned, peering sharply into the scraggly forest. "I know you're in there," he called fiercely, bending down to scoop up a rock. "You'd best come out so's I can see you."

Janey could hardly suppress a giggle as she stepped from behind a prickly rose bush. "It's all right, Lucas. I promise not to hurt you."

The boy looked puzzled for a moment. "How'd you know my name?"

"I was watching back there. I heard your dad calling you."

His blue eyes narrowed. "Are you one a them spies sent out to keep an eye on my pa?"

"Oh, no. I'm Ja...Jamie. Jamie Kane. I'm from the East. I just got here."

"I'm Lucas George," said the boy gravely, coming up to shake her hand. "Are you looking for land too?"

"Not me. I'm here by myself. I..."

"You're an all-over orphan? That's too bad." He looked at her sympathetically. "Me, I just lost my ma, but I still got my pa. That's why we're here." He turned, naturally assuming that Janey would fall in beside him. She did. The child barely reached Janey's elbow.

"I don't understand, Lucas. Why are you here?"

"Pa said he couldn't bear to live in Wyoming no more after Ma died. She was supposed to be givin' me a baby sister, but she died too. So we came here." He paused, then asked, "How come you're here?"

Janey wasn't sure young Lucas would understand about her mission, given the fact that she hardly understood it herself. Instead of answering, she asked the boy how old he was.

"Six. Almost seven, come June."

"What happened back there, with all those men?"

"It's about the land. Pa says there's lots of land out here. And since the government ain't sent out a surveyor, then it belongs to anyone that wants to settle on it." He looked up at Janey. "What's a surveyor?"

"It's someone who measures out land, I think, and makes it all official."

Lucas nodded as if that made sense. "Anyways, Pa says he's gonna build us a fine house with a place for his fiddle. He's gonna play it for me as soon as the house is finished." He frowned, trudging along the rutted, frozen path. "He ain't touched a string on that fiddle since before Ma died.

It'd sure be nice to hear him play again."

The wistfulness in his voice made Janey forget, momentarily, the cold seeping in through the bottoms of her runners. Unlike Lucas, she did, in fact, have two parents, even though one was halfway around the world. She suddenly felt a pang of sheepishness. Here was this poor little guy, coming all the way to Edmonton because he'd lost half his family and they were trying to make a new life. Meanwhile, Janey's mum could keep them afloat even if her dad lost his job. Compared to little Lucas, her troubles hardly counted.

"So, if you got no folk, how come you're here?" Lucas persisted.

"I think I might be able to help someone out here," she said finally. "You know how you sometimes get a feeling inside you about something?" Lucas nodded. "Well, I've got this feeling that I might stop something bad from happening."

The sound of an approaching horse and rider cut off the boy's reply. Janey and Lucas moved to the side of the path to let them pass.

A beautiful chestnut mare with a black mane and matching black socks cantered toward them. The rider, a middle-aged woman wearing buckskin leggings, a shawl, and a bonnet, nodded at them as she went by. She was almost gone from sight when the horse pulled up short, turned, and slowly cantered back. The woman peered intensely at Janey.

"Are you Jamie? Jamie from the East?"

Janey's heart leapt. How did anyone know she was here? She could only nod dumbly.

The woman in the saddle began to chuckle. Lucas looked

from the rider to Janey and back, especially as the chuckles escalated to roars of laughter.

"Mama was right!" the woman finally gasped, wiping her tears with the corner of her shawl. "She dreamed you'd be back, and here you are. That flannel shirt of yours has lasted a long time."

Janey felt shivers clambering up and down her spine. "Louisa?" she asked tentatively.

"Mrs. Louisa Black Bear," said the woman, dismounting and coming toward them, a huge smile lighting up her plump face.

A dozen thoughts and a jumble of emotions swirled inside Janey as she ran up to the short, round woman and hugged her fiercely. Here was someone who actually knew her; who might be able to help with her mission. And here, in her arms, was a grown female whom she'd just seen as a child – was it only a few weeks ago? Louisa'd been about the same age then as Lucas, and now here she was again, looking older than her own mother.

What had happened in the meantime? What about the letter? What about Louisa's father?

"Louisa, I have to know," she said, breaking the embrace to step back and look into the woman's eyes, which still twinkled as merrily as any mischievous seven-year-old's. "What happened to the letters? Did you join your father?"

Janey might have imagined the fleeting look of pain that shot across Louisa's eyes, but the woman turned briskly from Janey. "That's for a quieter time. Who is this young man here? A travelling companion?"

"I'm Lucas George, and me and my pa are building a new home back there," said the boy solemnly, offering his hand to shake. "Is you a woman with them breeches on?"

Louisa laughed again. "I am. Watch." She untucked some of the bulky material around her already generous waist and let it fall to the ground. Instantly she was dressed in an ankle-length skirt, with the leggings hidden demurely underneath.

"I can't ride properly with a skirt on," she explained, "but before I reach town I do this to look decent. Otherwise I'd scandalize the Reverend." She giggled, then looked at the pair. "I think I got the idea from you, Jamie."

Lucas looked puzzled, but before he could ask any questions, Louisa asked one of her own. "Want a ride into town? Blackfoot could carry all three of us."

Janey was grateful to be off the icy ground and nestled comfortably against Louisa's back. She was dying to ask more questions, but thought it might be better to wait until Lucas was out of earshot. Instead, she half-listened as Louisa questioned Lucas about the house his father was building, and marvelled at the fact that she was holding onto a woman who had, for Janey, just been a little girl. This must be what all those old people felt like who hadn't seen a kid in a few years. Granny must have felt like this when she saw me at the airport, Janey realized.

Her mind wandered. Old people must see an awful lot of stuff changing, she mused. Suddenly, she sat bolt upright. That old woman in the market! No wonder she knew me, she thought excitedly. That was Louisa! This Louisa! Louisa

Black Bear! I've met her before! I mean, even before the fort time!

Burbling with impatience, she hardly noticed that Louisa had reined the horse to a stop. "Louisa! Louisa, we have to talk."

"Not now, Jamie. I have an errand to run." Louisa slid down and unhitched her skirts from her waistband. Her passengers tumbled after her, then followed as she led the horse around a bend and onto a broad, rutted road. A motley assortment of wooden houses and false-fronted shops lined the avenue. One wagon lumbered past, wheels screeching. Church bells rang out over the scene, curiously empty of people except for a small crowd gathered in front of a two-storey building with the words J.A. McDougall's General Store grandly displayed in the two large front windows. Louisa hitched her horse, then headed toward the store. Just before Louisa reached the wooden sidewalk, Janey pulled her over.

"Um, Louisa? What year are we in?"

"I remember you asked Mama the same question," she said, turning to study Janey. "She said then that you were a child who had lost her way. I can see that now." Louisa's dark eyes penetrated Janey's. "It's 1882."

The woman was about to turn away when she stopped, and added, "In public I am called Mrs. Black Bear by almost all the white people in this place. You can do the same."

Janey fell back a step. Louisa's sparkling eyes might have been those of a little girl, but the lines around them were deep and creased and her body moved with the swaying dignity of a middle-aged woman. The mischievous little girl with the unstoppable tongue had become an adult who not only weighed her own words, but expected others to do the same.

THE MEN GATHERED IN FRONT OF THE STORE parted to let Louisa through to the door. Before she reached it, however, it flew open and a young, pretty woman dashed out, grabbing Louisa by the hands.

"Oh, Mrs. Black Bear! Did you find some? I've been so worried about my sweet little Alice. Wherever did you...? Oh, how foolish of me! Do come inside, please. Of course, the store's not open because it's Sunday, but I've been watching for you..." She bustled Louisa in, and Janey followed on her skirts, while Lucas planted himself on the boardwalk outside.

The store's interior was high-ceilinged and lined with display cases. Bolts of cloth, kitchen utensils, building tools, and canned food were stocked on shelves, while sacks of flour and seed were propped against them. A wood stove glowed cosily in the corner, where a small baby fretted in a cradle.

"I'm just so worried about her, Mrs. Black Bear. With my mother so far away, it's so hard..." The young woman's voice trailed away helplessly.

Louisa pulled a small, stoppered bottle from her pocket and handed it to the young woman. "Your baby will be just fine, Mrs. McDougall. Rub this oil on her chest every few hours and that will help. And give her lots to drink. The fever dries a baby up."

Mrs. McDougall clutched the bottle gratefully. "You've been so kind, Mrs. Black Bear. There are so few of us women here; I didn't know... Thank you."

Outside, Louisa waited until they'd passed the pipe smoke from the men gathered in front of the store before she turned to Janey. "Come and meet my husband. He'll be glad to see you again. We've both been waiting for you."

Lucas walked with them to where Blackfoot was hitched, saying that he would stay by the store to listen for news. Janey hardly noticed. She just wanted to get somewhere quiet so she could question Louisa about...well, everything.

BUT IT WAS ONLY LATER THAT EVENING, as the last of Louisa and Black Bear's children were tucked into bed in the rafters of their snug log house, that Janey finally got some answers. It was Black Bear who began.

"I knew you had magic when you disappeared in that hole," he said. "When I found out you had lured Martin Jameson into the water, I knew it was good magic."

"*I* didn't lure him into the water," Janey sputtered. "I was just helping and then I think he kicked me and I fell in and the letters all... What happened to him anyway?"

Black Bear grinned, turning to Louisa. "She talks as fast as you used to. I have forgotten."

Louisa rolled her eyes, but turned to Janey. "You mean Martin? He was fine, though some of the men had to go into the river and pull him out. He was not a good swimmer, you know. Even now he hates the water. And from that day on he had this awful red scar on his cheek that he said you gave him."

"What do you mean, 'even now'? Is Martin still here?" Janey asked anxiously.

"Martin Jameson is still here," said Black Bear. "He runs a farm south of the river."

Instantly Janey wondered whether those nasty brats who'd used her for target practice in 1907 were any relation. It'd be a hard question to ask, she decided. Instead, she asked another.

"The letters, Louisa, please tell me what happened to the letters."

Louisa sighed. "We had no word from Papa that night, or for many years later. When I was twelve, Mama told me that Papa had married another woman, a white woman, in the East, and that he was never coming back to get us. Maybe he wrote us and the letter was washed away when you fell in the water, or maybe he had forgotten us already when he stepped into the York boat that spring."

The quiet that followed was broken only by the crackling of the fire and the steady breathing of the children sleeping in the attic above. Black Bear gently covered his wife's hand with one of his own.

Janey's curiosity finally urged her on. "What happened then? Did you have to leave the fort?"

"We still lived there, but Mama worked hard; harder than before, and I did too. I made enough pemmican to fill ten York boats."

"When I watched you pound that dried meat into powder, I knew you were the wife for me," said Black Bear, a sly grin spreading over his face.

Louisa elbowed him playfully in the side. "And when

you promised to build me a cabin so I could farm while you went off hunting and trapping, I figured you'd be the husband for me."

Black Bear leaned into his wife. "Better even than that Mr. Martin Jameson?"

"That ugly old man! What would I want with him?"

Black Bear chuckled and sat back. "And I can still hunt better than he can."

"Didn't I tell you that he was boastful?" said Louisa, turning to Janey. "Besides, I didn't want to become Martin's country wife and have him go East whenever it suited him."

Again, Janey cut into the silence that followed. "You've learned English well," she said to Black Bear.

He nodded. "I've learned many things from the white men." His eyes narrowed briefly, but he continued. "I always wished I could have called to you that night by the fort. You were so frightened. I was just following to make sure you would be safe, and then you...were gone. I always wondered...where did you go when you went down that hole? And why are you here now?"

Janey sighed. What on earth should she tell them? Louisa leaned forward. "Tell us about your world, Janey. The one that you come from."

"Some of it will be yours too," said Janey finally. "I will meet you again, somewhere in the summer of 1907, I know that much."

Louisa nodded gravely. "Then I will grow to be an old woman. Will I see my children grow old around me?"

"I don't know. It will be such a short meeting. But I can

tell you that lots of people will move to Edmonton and that it will have many buildings and a bridge across the river..."

"Humph, that will put John Walter and his ferry out of business," said Black Bear.

"And there will be cars..." she caught Louisa's puzzled expression. "I mean automobiles..." Still nothing registered. "Carriages with engines...horseless carriages!" Janey was delighted when her small audience grasped her description. "And airplanes...machines that will carry people through the air! Oh, and telephones which will let people talk to each other from far away, and another machine that will let you see moving pictures...pictures of people and animals and things that are actually moving."

From the attic upstairs a voice called down softly: "Mama...Mama...is this all true?"

"Daniel, go to bed now. Right away." Louisa rose from the table.

"But Mama, imagine..."

"Not another word, Daniel. It's late." She turned back to Janey. "What you say is almost impossible to believe, and yet, part of me thinks..." A rustle from upstairs interrupted her. When it quieted, she whispered, "I think it's time for sleep. You are welcome to the bench here. I'll bring you blankets."

Before Janey drifted off, she realized she'd forgotten to tell Louisa that it was her words, about a disaster, that had driven Janey into the past. She must ask her about them tomorrow.

But Janey never got the chance. Early the next morning,

an insistent banging shook her awake. Black Bear was already at the door when Janey stuck her head out from the covers.

"Is...is Jamie there? I really need to see him," said a small child's voice.

Puzzled, Black Bear turned into the room. It took Janey a few seconds to realize that the child was asking for her; she'd forgotten about acting like a boy in front of her hosts. "I'm here, I'm here," she called, after sitting up and stuffing her cap on her head.

Black Bear beckoned the child inside, and Lucas edged past the tall Native man.

"Jamie, I'm so glad I found you. The men, they said they're getting ropes and goin' to Pa's property. Jamie, there's just him out there an' me, an'...an', you said..." Lucas seemed to run out of steam before he took a deep breath and began again. "You said...you *said* you were here to stop something bad from happening."

Janey had nearly forgotten all about the small boy who now stood shivering before her. She noticed that the toes of his shoes were worn through, and that his pants hardly reached his ankles. His hands were rough and callused, and his ears were as red as his cheeks.

Before she could ask where he'd spent the night, Louisa bustled forward with mugs of warm milk for them. Lucas clutched his gratefully, then took a long appreciative sip. Janey, who normally hated heated milk, recognized the rumbling in her stomach. She swallowed it quickly, then reached eagerly for a slice of buttered bread Louisa handed her.

"Quick, Jamie, please... Them men are looking mighty determined."

Louisa and Black Bear were exchanging words by the stove in Cree. As Louisa turned away, Black Bear switched to English. "It's not about us, Louisa. It's white men arguing over land now. Leave us out of it."

Louisa spoke again, and Black Bear finally sputtered, "Fine, take them. But stay out of it."

Children tumbled down from the attic, led by a young boy. "Can I come too, Mama?"

"No, Daniel." His father spoke sharply. "I need you with me on the north trapline today."

Dejected, the boy turned away, then sidled up to Janey. "Will there really be machines that can fly?" he whispered. Janey nodded, but before he could ask another question, Louisa had flung Janey a blanket to wrap about her and pushed her toward the door. Lucas danced in front of them on the path toward the stables, nervousness jittering through him. Louisa had to speak sharply to him before she could lead Blackfoot out of his stall.

In the early morning light, their breath left a trail behind them as they rode toward the main path. Once they found it, Louisa urged the horse into a trot, but slowed it down when she saw the crowd of men ahead. There were dozens of them, carrying sledgehammers and axes, with grim faces that gave Blackfoot's riders only cursory glances as the horse picked his way past on the frozen ground. Glimpsing a particular face, Janey shivered under her blanket. A long, red scar that started near one eye and ran down to the bottom of the nose seemed to glow furiously in the dawn light. The man's eyes caught Janey's.

"Whatcha starin' at, boy?" he said gruffly. Janey swung her eyes away, relieved that Blackfoot had overtaken the crowd, and could break out into a brisk trot again.

"Was that Martin?" she asked timidly.

Louisa nodded. "Mr. Jameson himself. I wouldn't cross paths with him again, if I were you. He has said many times that it was an unlucky day for him when a certain strange young boy came to the fort."

Janey gulped. She had no desire to even come near Martin again, especially now that he was a grown man with, what?...fifty years of bullying behind him. Not a chance. Janey shifted uncomfortably on the saddle, suddenly wondering why she was even on the horse, heading down this path.

"Louisa, why are these men so upset with Mr. George?"

Louisa sighed. "The land Mr. George is building his house on used to belong to Mr. Sinclair, but he sold it. The man who bought it isn't living on the land, so Mr. George just figured it was his to build on."

"That's why those men are so angry?"

"Well, they don't have any official papers for any of this land, because the government hasn't come out and measured it to tell anyone who it belongs to. Of course, when you think about it, it belonged to Black Bear's people before anyone else."

Janey felt squirmy inside. She'd studied some of this back at school, but it had never really sunk in until now. "Well, if these men behind us didn't really pay for the land, then..."

"Most of the men claimed the land after they stopped working for Edmonton House. They just agreed amongst themselves who owned what. If someone new comes in now and jumps their claims, it will make a mess of their system."

The framework of the little house appeared before them in the clearing. Mr. George was busy hammering away, and only looked up briefly when the horse approached.

"Pa! Pa! There are all these men comin', Pa! They got axes, and one man said he was gonna get a rope. Pa? They're not gonna, gonna..." his voice faltered.

Mr. George looked down at his son. "Hang me? Is that what you been thinkin'? There ain't no crime in wantin' to put up four walls and a roof, son. That rope ain't for hangin', though it might be for destroyin'." He looked at Louisa. "Thank ye kindly for bringin' my boy back."

Louisa climbed back onto Blackfoot. Panicking, Janey ran up to her. "Louisa, what am I supposed to do?"

"I am Mrs. Black Bear," she said, pulling herself up. "And this is your people's fight, not mine. You told the boy you must stop a terrible thing. Perhaps this is your destiny."

How would she know? thought Janey as she watched the woman ride away. Just as she rounded a corner, the first of the men came into view.

"George! You got no right to be building on this land," called one of the men.

"There ain't no law that says I can't," said Mr. George, edging toward the tent that huddled in the middle of the half-constructed building.

"The men in this community already know who owns

this land, and it ain't you, George," called another.

"Yeah, but the government hasn't said who owns it neither, so I reckon I can claim it just as well as any of you."

From the edge of the clearing, Janey and Lucas watched as more and more men poured in. "Every man from around these parts is here," whispered Lucas nervously.

A burly man elbowed his way toward the front of the crowd, which had now grown to more than one hundred onlookers. "George, if you do not remove this building from these premises in half an hour, these men here will be willing to render you all the assistance in their power. They'll knock it clear into the river if you don't see some sense."

Without turning his back to the crowd, Mr. George reached inside the open tent flap, then straightened again. "I ain't plannin' on movin' this building, and I'll shoot me the first man who tries," he said, and pointed a revolver at the burly man. The crowd fell silent for an instant, but as Lucas and Janey watched, a nimble farmer leapt through the studs behind Mr. George and knocked him down.

"I got the gun," yelled another man, and the crowd roared and surged forward.

"C'mon, Jamie. We gotta go help," shouted Lucas, scrambling around the crowd for an opening that would get him to his father. Janey followed reluctantly, uncertain of what she should do. If this was the disaster she was supposed to stop, she didn't have a clue about how to do it. Reaching the upright studs of the building, she watched as at least four men tried to pry Mr. George from the frame of his house, with little success. He had wrapped arms and legs around the sturdiest of the studs, and looked for all the world like a firefighter about to drop down his pole.

Little Lucas darted frantically between the men, blindly pulling at their coats and kicking at their ankles. He was crying, Janey saw, and when a fierce-looking man grabbed him by the collar and shook the small child, Janey did the only thing she could. An ear-splitting whistle pierced through the clearing, and everyone turned to stare at her.

"Now, now, look," said Janey, making her way forward and snatching Lucas from the stranger. "There has to be some sensible way to solve this." She had no idea about what she should say, but figured that as long as she could speak, the crowd might not do anything drastic. Besides, if it worked in 1907, it ought to work in 1882.

She turned to face the glowering men. Somewhere along the way she'd lost Louisa's blanket, and a sudden gust of wind made her shiver in her flannel shirt and overalls. "There's so much land out here that you can't just wreck a man's house for no reason," she urged. She ignored the mutterings and continued. "This man's just trying to build a home for himself and his son, just like all of you."

"Who are you to tell us?" came a growl from the right side of the crowd. Janey swung toward the voice, and realized, to her horror, that she was looking into Martin's scarred and angry face.

"Yeah, well? Who are ya?" Martin advanced on Janey as she backed away. "I know ya, don't I? I been watchin' ya and yer a troublemaker if I ever knew one." He grabbed hold of her arm and muttered, more quietly, "Same shirt, same eyes, same funny shoes. I don't know how ya did it, but you're that same lazy, spiteful good-for-nothin' come back to cause me more trouble. Well, not this time." His voice rose and he turned to face the men.

"Boys, this here's a troublemaker of the first sort and it was probably all his idea. What are we waitin' for? Get the rope."

Eager hands pushed the long coils of rope over the crowd and toward the studs. Terrified, Janey closed her eyes. "Thinkin' you might deserve this, aren't ya?" said Martin close to her ear. He yanked her out of the house frame. She opened her eyes to watch as men tied the rope to the studs, and started pulling.

"Pa! Pa!" cried Lucas, his voice thin and high-pitched in terror. Mr. George still clung to his stud, and with every yank of the house, he seemed to settle more firmly around the wood.

Grunting, swearing, and sweating, the throng pushed the little house frame to the cliff's edge. "Ya better get out, George," said one of the men. "This is goin' over."

"Then let me get my tent and our bedrolls," said Mr. George, resignedly. His little tent had already collapsed; he folded it together in four quick movements, scooped up the bundle, and stepped gracefully from his house.

"Let's go, boys," shouted Martin, and with one final, grunting heave, the house crashed over the side of the cliff. While most of the men cheered, others flung the extra lumber after the demolished house.

"Now it's your turn," said Martin. Before she could turn,

or struggle, or even shout, he picked Janey up and flung her over the side of the cold, snowy embankment. It was only as she was tumbling down, feeling the icy slush soak through her overalls, that fury took hold, and Janey thrashed around wildly, hoping to break her fall. But nothing worked. Exhausted, bruised, and dizzy, Janey finally landed in a puddle of slush at the bottom.

Please, please let this be present-day time, thought Janey before she opened her eyes. But the cold water seeping into the front of her overalls made her panic. It had been hot and dry in her own time. What if she was stuck in 1882?

CHAPTER SEVEN

SHE COULDN'T, SHE JUST COULDN'T, OPEN HER EYES AND face those awful men anymore. Maybe if she lay here quietly on this cold, wet riverbank, everyone would go away and she could find a way to get back, thought Janey. She was obviously in the wrong time period. And she'd been absolutely no help to Lucas. If anything, the sight of her had goaded Martin on. But what *was* she supposed to be doing here, in a muddy little town with a guy who had decided she was his arch-enemy? And how was any of this supposed to help her keep from moving to Edmonton?

A whimper rose to Janey's lips, but she swallowed it back down. All right, Janey, she said to herself; you can lie here feeling sorry for yourself or you can pull yourself together, get out of this puddle, and face the world. Drawing her arms under her, she felt the earth shift. Janey's eyes flew open and there, beside her, was Granny's locket, dangling off a button on her flannel cuff. She grabbed it, and sat up.

Oh joy! Oh joy! She was back at the construction site. Rain pelted down, making her colder and wetter with every second's passing. But the seconds belonged to this century, and not to some period in the past. Janey stood up stiffly, lumbered over to the fence, and clambered over.

The ride back in the storm felt like she was peddling at least twice her weight in water. By the time she reached home, she was convinced that every eyelash, every button-hole thread, and every last bit of her sneaker laces were soaked through and through.

As soon as she swung open the garage door, Janey noticed that Marilyn was missing. Dust motes hung motionless in the shaft of odd light that trickled in through the raindrops on the garage window. Had something happened to Granny?

She dropped her bike, flung off her grandfather's clothes, and ran toward the house. The sight of Granny standing at the kitchen window almost made Janey falter. Instead, she opened the back door.

"Granny! Marilyn's gone!"

"I'm not surprised, kiddo. Your dad took her out to look for you."

Janey faltered. Oh, yeah. Her dad. She'd almost forgotten about him in the rush of everything that had just happened.

"Did he...I mean, was he mad at me?"

"The weather's bad, Janey, and he was worried. *I* was worried," said Granny, handing Janey a towel. "I know you're getting to be a big girl, but you can't be taking off without letting someone know where you are." Granny's voice, uncharacteristically sharp, made Janey look up at the thin woman who had turned away to pour a cup of tea. The bright red kerchief on her grandmother's head made Janey think of the one she'd worn at Edmonton House. But this one hid hardly any hair at all.

Her grandmother poured a cup of tea and moved toward the living room. "Come sit with me, kiddo. I got stuff I need to talk to you about."

Janey changed out of her wet clothes, then snuggled up beside her grandmother.

"I hear your dad told you about him losing his job and you guys maybe moving out here," Granny began.

Janey blinked, but said nothing.

"He didn't tell you the whole story." She took a sip from her tea. "I've gotta go in for an operation. It's that cancer. The operation's kind of an iffy procedure. And if I make it, it's going to take a long time before I'm back on my feet."

Janey blinked again. What did Granny mean, *"if* I make it"? What was going on here? She was about to interrupt, but Granny went on.

"I'm telling you all this because I think you were brought out here under false pretences. You're growing up, and if you're going to make a decision you need to have all the facts. I don't want you moving here with any kind of illusions. This place will be a sick house for a while."

"Granny," said Janey, her voice small. "What do you mean, *'if* you make it'?"

"Oh, kiddo, when you get to my age, a lot can go wrong on the operating table. It probably won't, but it's a possibility. A real possibility." She took another sip of her tea.

"But...Granny!" Janey's voice caught in her throat. Tears collected and threatened to spill down her cheeks.

Granny put down her tea and gathered her tearful grand-daughter in her arms. "There now, there now. It's all right. This old body of mine has survived all kinds of calamities, and one more is just...one more."

"But Granny...this is so...so unfair." She was wailing now, tears soaking into her grandmother's T-shirt.

"It's just life, kiddo. But I'll tell you something. Since you've been out here, you've been making me feel...I don't know, as if I can make it. Maybe it's just all that youthful energy of your rubbing off on me. But it's sure been good having you around."

They sat quietly for a moment. "When's the operation?"

"Next Tuesday."

Janey counted. Four days. Four lousy days left. She started crying even louder. "But Granny, that's only four days to...to..." Janey's mind went blank.

"To teach you how to play rummy properly? You bet. Go get the cards."

"Oh, no, Granny. Not now. Tell me something instead. Tell me...tell me about Grampa. About how you met."

"You don't want to hear that old story, do you?" said Granny, fumbling in her pocket until she'd found a clean tissue to give to Janey. Janey blew her nose and nodded. Granny finished her tea and settled in against the sofa. The black, roiling storm clouds darkened the room, but the light from the street lamp caught the raindrops on the window.

Janey snuggled in against her grandmother, watching idly as the drops tracked down the pane, and listening to the steady thump, thump of her grandmother's heart.

"Well. It was just after the war, and I was pretty old by then, maybe twenty-two, and still no steady boyfriend," began Granny.

"That's not very old. Mummy says I'm not even allowed to think of marrying before I'm twenty-five."

"We did things differently then. Anyway, I'm walking along Jasper Avenue in the spring and there's this nice breeze picking up the scent of lilacs and the sun is out. I'm wearing my red-and-white striped, second-best dress and my new red shoes that pinch my toes but make me look really good. And I'm minding my own business and suddenly the door of the tailor shop beside me swings open and this fella steps out onto the sidewalk and just about squashes my foot."

In spite of herself, Janey started to giggle. "Was that Grampa?"

"Course it was. Large as life, dressed in the best suit money could buy – he'd just got out of the army – and there he was, stomping all over my foot."

"What did you do? Scream at him?"

"No! I almost fainted with the pain. Those shoes really were dreadfully tight, but oh, they made me look so good. Still, when your grandfather practically jumped on them..."

"So what did you do, Granny?"

"Well, like I said, I almost fainted, and he had to grab hold of me, and...that was that."

"It wasn't exactly sweeping you off your feet, was it?"

"Stomping them off was more like it. But he used to say, 'Amanda Logan, I'd been hunting for you in that red-and-white dress just about all my life. I only stepped on your toes so you wouldn't run away from me.'" Granny chuckled.

"We had such good times together." She paused, remembering. "You know, he was really, really excited when you were born. In fact, I think it was him who suggested we call you Janey. It's too bad you two never met. He'd have loved to see you now."

"He was born somewhere else, wasn't he?"

"Yup. His family was from Ukraine and his parents died when he was a kid. An uncle, I think, brought him over here. He seemed to have lost contact with him by the time I came into the picture. But there was an Edmonton family he knew that he kept in touch with for quite some time."

"Is that where he got the name Kane? It seems a bit short for a Ukrainian name."

"Grampa shortened it when he was in the army. He was tired of people making a mess of the proper pronunciation. Besides, I liked being Mrs. Kane. Gave me an excuse to buy extra candy canes at Christmas."

The kitchen screen door slammed, and Janey's dad appeared. "I see you're back, Janey," he said, hanging an old raincoat by the door before he turned to look at her.

Janey rose from Granny's side and went to face her dad. "I'm sorry, Daddy. I shouldn't have left you like that. And I'm really sorry about your job." When he held out his arms to hug her, Janey stepped gratefully into his embrace. "You're the best," she whispered in his ear.

"Okay, you two, break it up. Did you bring something home to eat, Alex?" asked Granny, pushing herself off the couch. "I'm suddenly famished."

"Good," said her dad, hauling groceries into the kitchen. "Tonight's menu includes pasta primavera and fresh garden salad. Or, if that doesn't sit well with the ladies, Chef Kane can scramble up some omelettes."

THE RAIN HAD STOPPED by the next morning, and Janey was outside checking to see if the sunflowers had survived the storm when her father came up beside her, a mug of coffee in his hand.

"Grampa had this complicated way of staking those flowers; I'm going to see if I can remember," he said.

"I'm not sure it's going to be worth it," said Janey finally. She'd slept badly, waking several times when thunder and lightning seemed to rip through her room. The weather mirrored her thoughts, which dashed between worries about her grandmother and the agony of leaving Toronto.

"What do you mean, Janey?"

"Granny might not make it and then it just wouldn't be worth it, would it?"

"Honey, it's just as likely that she will, and then she'd have these beautiful flowers to cheer her on."

"What happens if she doesn't die and we don't move back here?" Janey finally asked.

"Well, in that case she'd have to go into a nursing home for a while, and she'd feel uncomfortable about leaving the house empty for that long. It might be time for her to sell it. Even with the students around, it's a big job for her."

"What's Mummy say about all this?"

"Oh, she's happy to do whatever we decide. It looks as if she's going to be getting another assignment anyhow, so she won't be in Canada lots, whether it's Toronto or Edmonton."

They were silent for a bit, watching a magpie chase a neighbour's cat down the back lane.

"But if Granny dies, we wouldn't have to move here, would we?" asked Janey, when the bird and the cat had disappeared.

"Well, that's one way of looking at it," said her dad, turning back toward the house.

"I didn't mean... Dad!" she called after him. The screen door banged shut behind him.

On the day of the operation everyone was up early. Because Granny hadn't been allowed to eat anything since the day before, she took a long bath while Janey and her dad had breakfast.

The two hardly spoke to each other, and had been uncommonly silent over the last few days. Her dad had been busy painting and fixing up stuff around the house. "I'm getting it ready in case we have to sell," he'd told Janey curtly. In the evenings he disappeared into his old bedroom in the basement. Even Granny was quieter than usual, choosing to spend her time under the lilac bushes in the backyard.

It had taken Janey the past two days to come to a decision. She'd realized, finally, that the disaster she was meant to prevent had nothing to do with her, or with Anna or Lucas or even Louisa. The connection had always been Granny's locket, and somehow, if Janey was to stop anything bad from happening, it had to do with Granny, who would have been a little girl called Amanda Logan back in the 1920s. That was the only era at Fort Edmonton Park that she hadn't yet visited – in the past – and it was the one in which she was sure she could prevent something horrible from happening. Deep inside, Janey felt that if she could do this, then somehow Granny would survive her operation.

As her dad swallowed the last of his orange juice, Janey announced, "I'm not going with you to the hospital this morning. I'd rather go to Fort Edmonton Park."

He stared at her for a moment. Granny came up behind her son and put her hand on his shoulder. "What a good idea, Alex. I don't want her sitting around that gloomy old hospital on such a glorious summer day. You can pick her up later this afternoon, and then both of you can come and see me when I'm more coherent."

"Yeah, sure. Good idea. We'll drop you off," said Janey's dad.

"Oh, that's okay. I've got the bike and this way you don't have to come back for me. I'll be fine, Dad. And I'll be here by, when? Four?"

"That'll be just fine, kiddo," said Granny, coming over to Janey's side of the table. "I think it's time we went, Alex. That toast is looking mighty tempting. Janey, can you get my bag from my bedroom?"

hiking socks, and shoved those in her pack too.

She was the first one through the gate when the park opened. Ten minutes later she was at the fence. An instant later, she was underground. And this time, there was only one tunnel. Pushing, shoving, and sweating, she wedged her way into the small shaft, and struggled up to the surface.

When she emerged, the air was colder than anything she'd ever imagined, and the world was white.

CHAPTER EIGHT

THE VAST EXPANSE OF SNOW SURROUNDING JANEY sparkled with a cold, clear brilliance that took her breath away. Truly, she could barely breathe, because the frosty air seemed to pinch her nostrils shut whenever she inhaled through her nose. She reached into the pocket of her pea coat, pulled out the white silk scarf, and wrapped it over her face.

As her eyes adjusted to the frozen landscape, she realized she'd come up on a flat, open plain. In the distance, specks of black crept along with ant-like slowness. Squinting, Janey made out small, old-fashioned cars. Her heart leapt. She must have made it to the right era!

The cold chased her along the road, forcing her to break into a run just to keep warm. If this is what Edmonton's like in the winter, maybe Granny should move to Toronto with us, thought Janey grimly. She reached an intersection at the

same time as an old-style truck puttered up from the opposite direction. It turned left, skidding wildly. Janey heard a
thump and a groan before its driver found the right gear and
drove on toward the rest of the vehicles. Another groan
forced Janey's eyes back to the intersection.

A boy almost as big as Janey was rising from the side of
the road, dusting the snow off his sweater. "I almost got all
the way there!" he said, grinning amicably at her.

"All the way where?"

"To Blatchford Field, of course!" The boy looked at
Janey's puzzled face. "Wop May an' Vic Horner? Haven't ya
heard? They're flyin' off today, way up to Fort Vermilion –
that's more 'n 600 miles north a here, an' it's minus 33
degrees. Where've ya been these last few days? It's been all
over the radio."

The boy fell into step in the wheel rut next to Janey's.
With no mittens or overcoat, he set an even brisker pace
than Janey had earlier.

"I haven't heard. I've just come from...away from here."
She switched the topic of conversation from herself. "What's
so special about this Wop what's-his-name? Why's he flying
up there?"

"They've never flown that far in such cold weather before.
But there's a diphtheria outbreak up in Fort Vermilion an' Wop
May an' Vic Horner said they'd fly the medicine up. They
called it the an-ti-toxin on the radio." The boy savoured the
word slowly, repeating it under his breath as he jogged along.

Unaccustomed to running in freezing temperatures, Janey
had to slow down. "But couldn't they just get it up there

some other way?" she asked, hoping her new companion would slow down too. "A truck or something?"

The boy looked at her momentarily, and Janey was struck by how similar his hazel eyes were to her own. "A truck?" he said scornfully. "In this weather? With all this snow? They'd be lucky if they could get dogsleds to bring it up, but it would take weeks! By that time whole towns could be wiped out."

They had reached the first of the parked vehicles, and more and more cars were pulling up behind them. "C'mon, we're almost there," said the boy, picking up speed again.

"Hey, wait a minute! What's your name?" Janey called.

The boy stopped and turned again. "I'm Oleksiy. An' who are you, besides not knowing about the biggest thing that's ever happened in Edmonton?"

"I'm Jamie," said Janey, puffing alongside.

"Well, I'm pleased to meet you, Jamie, but now could we hurry so we can get to the airfield?"

He pushed through a huge crowd of people milling about near a rickety wooden building.

"Not so fast, buddy." A huge, uniformed figure stepped in front of Oleksiy.

"But...but I just wanna watch Mr. May take off."

"You an' everyone else, buddy. C'mon, stay behind the fence. The less of you whippersnappers on the runway, the easier it'll be for Mr. May to take off."

"But..."

Janey tugged at Oleksiy's arm. She'd spotted a side door into the rickety hangar. If they got into the building, it might open out onto the runway. And even if it didn't, it would be a darn sight warmer than it was out here.

Oleksiy grumbled as Janey pulled him away, but when she opened the door of the hangar and slipped inside, he followed her quietly. The sudden gloom after the brilliant light made them both stop in their tracks until their eyes adjusted. Then Oleksiy broke the silence with an excited whisper. "That's the *Edmonton,* the one Mr. May flew under the High Level Bridge last summer. Ain't she a beauty?"

He ran his hand along the body of the small aircraft, caressing the struts that supported the wings. Janey stared at the plane, amazed. It looked for all the world like one of those First World War fighter planes; the kind that been in those great battles with the Red Baron over the English Channel.

As if he'd heard her thoughts, Oleksiy said, "You know Wop May helped bring down the Red Baron, don't you? He got a medal for it."

"Oh, is he going to fly up there in this thing? It doesn't even have a roof for the pilot."

"Nah, he's not flying this one. He says they're gonna take the Avro Avian. But it doesn't have a roof over the cockpit either. Who ever heard of such a thing?"

"Well, it would certainly keep the pilot warmer," said Janey, tired of looking like she didn't know a thing. "How are those two supposed to fly when it's minus 33 or whatever you said? It's gonna be even colder up there with the wind against them; they'll never make it if they've got to fly such a long distance."

"But that's why the whole thing's so exciting," said Oleksiy, his voice rising. "Nobody's ever really flown up there before. They hardly have any runways, and the snow could make it hard for them, but they'd be saving hundreds of lives. And if they make it, they'll be heroes. Don't you know anything?"

"Yeah, well, *I* know they're gonna have planes with roofs over their cockpits; they're probably working on 'em right now," said Janey heatedly.

"Okay, you two. What are you up to back here?" A stocky man, made bulkier by at least two sweaters and a jacket, appeared from the back of the plane. "And what do you mean, they're gonna have these planes with roofs on 'em?"

Oleksiy was backing away. "C'mon, Jamie, we'd better get outta here."

"No! Wait!" The man grabbed Janey's coat. "Jamie what? What's your last name, you?" He tugged her toward him. She caught sight of Oleksiy hovering by the open door, waiting for her to escape.

"What's it to ya?" said Janey, mustering all the bravado she could and trying to break free.

The man was peering at her intently. "It's not Kane, is it?"

The sound of her last name made Janey freeze. She peered at the man closely. The fact that there was no sign of a scar made her a little less apprehensive. "Who are you?" she asked, puzzled.

"I'm Daniel, Louisa Black Bear's son."

Janey stood transfixed. The child in the rafters, who

couldn't get to sleep on the night she was there, now stood before her, a middle-aged man with silver in his hair. He grinned at her.

"I remember you tellin' about the phones and the horse-less carriages and the planes, and now, here it all is," he said.

Oleksiy had stepped back into the building and was circling the pair. "What's all this about, Jamie? Whaddya talkin' about?"

Janey shook the memory of Louisa and Black Bear's snug cabin from her mind, and turned to Oleksiy. "I think I've found us a way to get onto the runway, Oleksiy. This is Daniel Black Bear, the son of an old...friend of mine. Sorry Oleksiy, I don't think I know your last name."

"It's Kanasewich," said the boy, shaking the man's hand.

"And my last name's different now, Jamie. It's been just Black since I started working here. It was easier."

Janey was dying to ask about Louisa, but Oleksiy cut in. "So, can you get us out there before they take off?"

Daniel nodded, and motioned them to follow through the large doors at the end of the building.

"Tell me about your mum, Daniel. How is she?" said Janey, scurrying to stay out of her companion's earshot.

"She's not with us any more. She died just after I got back from the war," said Daniel, pulling his jacket tighter around him.

Janey was quiet a moment. The lively child, the competent mother, and the sharp-tongued old woman all flashed through her mind. Janey had so many questions for her, and now she was gone. "I'm sorry, Daniel."

"She led a good life, and she lived with me and my wife at the end, so that was all right. I got a girl called Louisa. And a boy called James." He smiled at her. "She talked about you a lot, especially near the end. She knew you would come back. Are you back now, or is this your real time?"

"Oh, this is just a visit, I hope. My real time's even further ahead."

"Can you tell me what'll be happening then?" Daniel turned to Janey, and she could see Louisa's inquisitive spark in his dark eyes.

"I'll try, but can I first see this guy with the funny name fly off with the medicine?"

"You mean Wop May? Yeah, I don't suppose his parents thought it would turn out this way when they named him after old Wilfrid Laurier."

"Who?"

Oleksiy, who'd been trying not to eavesdrop, burst out: "You know! The prime minister before the war. Don't they teach you anything out East?"

"The same," said Daniel, grinning. "Wop is just short for Wilfrid. Wop says it was better than being named after John Sparrow David Thompson, the fella not too long before Laurier."

"Sparrow'd be good, since he flies so much," said Oleksiy, laughing.

"How come you know so much about him, Daniel? I mean, Mr. Black?" asked Janey.

"I'm one of the mechanics here. You put all those ideas into my head, Jamie, that night in the attic, and I just kept following these machines." He nodded at the tiny airplane in front of them, surrounded by a crowd of people milling about and stomping their feet against the cold.

It was an old-fashioned biplane, with two sets of wings covered with cloth, painted grey and held together with wire cables. "The wingspan's twenty-eight feet and it'll cruise at sixty miles an hour," said Daniel proudly. If you park two modern cars nose to nose, that's about the distance from wingtip to wingtip, thought Janey. She went up to the side of the plane and ran her mitten along the G-CAVB lettering.

"What's that kid doin' there? An' this one over here?" Somebody grabbed the collar of Janey's jacket and yanked her back.

"It's all right, Jameson, these two are here with me," said Daniel, putting a protective hand on Janey's arm.

"Yeah? Well, just make sure they don't wreck anything," said the man, giving Janey a final shake before letting her go. She turned to look as the man stomped away, grumbling.

"That Jameson. Always sticking his nose into things. Keeps trying to run for city council, but the voters won't have him," said Daniel, watching the retreating figure go up to a group of reporters. "I bet he figures if he comes out here it'll make him look good."

Janey watched a well-dressed man brandishing a lit cigar shake hands with anyone who'd let him. She knew that he wasn't the same Jameson who'd made her life miserable before. This guy was younger, but maybe he was related. She asked Daniel.

"Oh yeah, I seem to remember my mother mentioning something about you and old man Jameson," he said. "He's long dead, but this guy's a grandson. Looks like he's cut from the same cloth."

Memories of her last meeting with Martin surged through Janey. "Hey, Da...Mr. Black, whatever happened to George Lucas? Do you remember? When I was there, they were pitching his dad's house into the river valley."

"Yeah, there was something like that when you were here last," said Daniel. "I think they packed up and moved away. We never heard anything more about them."

As they spoke, a car nosed its way through the crowds and spluttered to a stop in front of the aircraft. A man stepped out, bearing a box wrapped in a plaid blanket and tied with a string.

"You've got to keep this warm, May," he said, handing it to a man bundled up in a fur coat. Flying goggles glinted from the top of his leather pilot's hood.

"Yes sir, Dr. Bow. The charcoal burners are already lit in the baggage compartment. They'll be snug and warm there."

Janey's fingers were numb with cold and she could hardly feel her toes. How could he possibly keep anything warm in an open-cockpit airplane made with some sheets of canvas and a few bales of wire? She peeked into the airplane. Why – the burners were hardly bigger than the barbecue her dad set up for picnics.

She stared at the man shaking hands with well-wishers on the field. He was probably younger than her dad, but not by much. When he smiled at someone, he had a friendly, amiable sort of face, but under that huge buffalo coat and tiny flying helmet he hardly looked the tall, dark, and handsome hero type.

"Ain't this just the most exciting thing, Jamie?" Oleksiy had come up and clapped her on the back. She nodded, watching May do up his coat, pull up his collar, and tug down his goggles. He wrapped a thick, woollen scarf around his neck and tucked the ends inside. Janey's own neck began to itch in sympathy. She hoped he wasn't allergic to wool, the way she was. He'd be scratching and itching for the next 600 miles. He could really use one of those cool ski masks they've got now, she thought, or at least something soft under all that wool. Her mittened fingers rose to the silk scarf she'd taken from her grandfather's trunk.

Impulsively, she pulled it off and ran over. "Mr. May! Mr. May! Here." She thrust the scarf into his gloved hands.

"What's this for, kid?" Wop May turned from the reporters and onlookers to examine the delicate piece of white silk.

Janey grew embarrassed. She was acting like one of those stupid groupies at a rock concert, flinging bits of clothing at the stars. She hardly knew what to say.

"It looks like it's silk, Wop," said one of the men at his elbow. "I read somewhere that you could put that against your mouth and your breath wouldn't freeze up against your skin. You oughta take it."

Wop pulled one hand out of his glove and fingered the flimsy material. "Thanks, kid," he said, looking Janey in the eyes.

"I hoped, I hope..." She felt quite flustered. "At least it'll make your wool scarf less scratchy." As he turned away, she asked desperately, "You don't know an Amanda Logan, do you?"

"Can't say's I do. But thanks for the scarf." He turned. "Let's go, Vic. It's not getting any warmer."

While the two pilots climbed into the plane, Daniel had Janey and Oleksiy stand by each wheel. "When I signal, you remove the chocks," he told them.

Janey grabbed Daniel's sleeve. "What chocks?"

"The pieces of wood under the wheels," said Daniel, before the sound of an engine catching cut him off.

With a thumbs-up sign from May, Daniel gave the propeller blade a mighty heave. The crowd cleared the runway and Daniel signalled Janey and Oleksiy. They removed the chocks and the plane lurched forward. It scooted along the snowy runway and then it was airborne, a disappearing grey speck in a cold winter sky.

"Wasn't that somethin'? Wasn't that just the best thing? Boy, I hope they make it." Oleksiy was clapping his arms against his sides and jumping up and down. Janey realized it had less to do with excitement and more with the cold. As she watched the plane vanish, she felt oddly deflated. Something, some odd feeling, told her that this moment had been important. But she couldn't quite put her finger on it, and the boy's babbling was distracting her. So was the cold. She felt it seeping into her jacket and through the soles of her feet. How much colder it must be for the two pilots flying straight into the north wind.

Oleksiy interrupted her thoughts. "You don't have anything to eat in one of those nice warm pockets, do you?"

Janey shook her head. "Yeah, I'm hungry too. I wonder if Daniel, I mean, Mr. Black, has anything to eat."

But Jameson was dragging Daniel over to the press. "They just want to get a shot of us together," he said, leading them to a group armed with pencils, pads, and microphones. Then as Janey and Alex watched, a reporter bundled Daniel into a car and drove away, leaving Jameson waving his fist at the retreating vehicle. "Those *Journal* newshounds will do anything to get a scoop," muttered a bystander, as the other reporters ran off to their own vehicles.

"I think we'd better head into town too," said Oleksiy, watching the crowds clear. "Where do you live, anyway?"

"Me? Well, I just got here, so I don't really have a place..."

"You're like me, then. Did you run away too?"

"Run away? 'Course not. I just..." She thought of her grandmother in the hospital, probably being operated on right now. Her dad sitting on one of those awful, uncomfortable plastic chairs, or pacing the long hallways. "I just came here to do something."

"Well, if it was to watch the plane take off, that's already happened. They won't be back until tomorrow earliest. We'd better find us someplace warm."

He eyed the cars and trucks pulling away from the airport. "There, look. If we grab on the back of that truck there, we might get somewhere. Let's go."

A truck with horizontal wooden slats surrounding its bed was just pulling away from the road. Janey ran as hard as she could, and caught at the slats. That was the easy part. Pulling her feet up, so they were resting on the truck's bumper, instead of dragging on the road, was much harder. Oleksiy must have had practice at this sort of thing. He was already in the truck bed, and he helped haul her over the slats. They clambered forward through gunny sacks to sit, backs propped against the cab, out of sight of the driver.

The odd, nagging feeling Janey'd had as the plane took off hadn't disappeared. She watched the hangar shrink into the white landscape, and wondered whether she should be leaving the airport. Each time she'd entered into the past, it had been through the site of the future airport hangar. There was something about the airplane, or the airport, or the flight that was connected with her.

Perhaps she was done. Perhaps her mission, to stop something terrible from happening, had already taken place. But she'd done nothing yet, except talk to Daniel and learn that Louisa had died, give Wop May a silk scarf, and remove the chocks. How was any of that supposed to help? So maybe he'd stay a little bit warmer and a little less itchy on his flight to save hundreds of lives. Big deal. That couldn't have been why she was here.

She sighed. On top of everything else, how was she supposed to get back to her real time? Before, it had always kind of happened to her. What was she supposed to do now, fling herself off the riverbank or find some kind of hole to jump into?

The truck was gearing down and turning. Oleksiy looked worried. He motioned her to cover herself with some of the gunny sacks. The vehicle sputtered down a long driveway and stopped. A door clanked open, and moments later, they could hear rusty hinges squealing in the cold. The truck door banged shut and the vehicle moved slowly forward. The engine cut out and, in the silence, Janey and Oleksiy hardly breathed.

"Hello, girls," a woman called as she climbed out of the truck's cab. "I'll be out to see you after I've changed into Eric's overalls."

Another squeal of hinges and a large door banged shut. Suddenly it was dark and much quieter. Janey and Oleksiy lay there an extra minute in silence, then sat up at the same time.

"Cows," said Oleksiy, sniffing the air. "That's good, and bad."

"Why's it bad?" Janey asked in the darkness.

"They don't like me. That's one of the reasons I left my uncle's farm. How was I supposed to milk the cows when they kept trying to kick me?"

"So why's it good?"

"Milk. They've got it, and it's warm. And it means we're in a barn with lots of hay, where we can sleep tonight. I was hoping we'd get into the city by this evening, but maybe this is better."

Janey grew suspicious. "How are we supposed to get the milk if they keep trying to kick you?"

"I ain't gonna milk 'em. You are," said Oleksiy with an air of finality, jumping from the truck bed. "Take a couple of these gunny sacks with you. It'll make the hay itch less."

"Wait a minute! I've never milked any cows! How do you expect me to..."

"A city boy, eh? I bet you think milk just appears by magic in glass bottles in the milkman's cart."

Ha! thought Janey. Wait until he finds out about plastic bags and cardboard containers. She eyed the creatures staring at them over the sides of a large stall.

Oleksiy had dropped his sack by a ladder and collected a bucket and milking stool by the door.

"Here," he said. "Climb over with the bucket and try that one over there; she looks like she's got the most to give."

Now that her eyes had adjusted to the dark, Janey could see the steam erupting from four pairs of large nostrils.

"Uh-uh," said Janey, backing away. "Those are big, big creatures. I'm not goin' in there. Are you crazy?"

Oleksiy sighed. "If you don't, then we'll spend the night with empty stomachs, which will make it a lot harder to forget the cold. C'mon. They look like nice cows."

"If they look that nice, you go in and milk 'em. At least you know how to do it."

Oleksiy sighed again, grabbed the bucket and stool, and swung over the boards. As he landed, a calf started up from the hay bed and skittered over to one side. One of the cows took several steps toward the boy.

"Easy now, easy now," said Oleksiy. Another cow started forward from the opposite direction. The calf began bawling.

"Here now. Easy now," said the boy again. Janey couldn't help but notice his voice breaking at the end of every sentence. The cows did not look easy. Suddenly, the cow with the calf swung her body around, so Oleksiy was shoved against the barn wall. The stool clattered against the boards, and the boy called out: "Jamie! Get the farmer. I'm in trouble."

Get the farmer!? And get caught!? Janey reached over the boards, picked up the stool by one leg, and brought the seat down on the cow's rump. The cow moved away grudgingly, and Oleksiy bolted out, nearly barrelling Janey down as he leapt over the boards.

Over the animals' uneasy mooing, Janey could hear him mutter, "I hate cows, I hate cows. I hate..." He was cut short by barking outside. Oleksiy stiffened. "Quick! Up the ladder!" He scooped up the sacks and scurried out of sight. Janey had just enough time to put the stool and bucket back before she clambered up as well.

The door opened, revealing a weak rectangle of winter light.

"Hush now, girls! Hush! What is it?" Swaddled in a man's overcoat and gumboots, a woman stepped into the light, then swung the door shut behind her.

"Shh now! Hush!" The mooing subsided as the woman entered the corral and went softly from one animal to the next. Finally she plunked herself down on the stool and Janey heard the sizzling hiss of milk rhythmically hitting the bottom of the pail. Efficient with her movements, the woman finished the milking, quickly fed and watered the animals, and stepped back through the door. No more light came from outside. The afternoon had disappeared.

"Well, that does it," said Oleksiy, rolling over onto his back in the hay. "We'll have to spend the night here and hope we can hitch a ride out tomorrow – if she decides to go anywhere."

He started burrowing into the straw, pulling a gunny sack with him to use as a pillow. Janey watched in the gloom, then did the same. She was surprised by how warm she soon felt, but it wouldn't allow her to fall asleep.

"So, where are you really from?" came Oleksiy's voice in the darkness.

"I'm from the East, like I said. Toronto. Where are you from?"

"I'm from a farm – my uncle's farm – west of here. I heard about the Mercy Flight – that's what they're callin' it on the radio – and just wanted to come see it. My uncle said it was a fool's errand and nothin' to waste gas on, and that the plane'd probably fly right over the farm, so why bother goin'?"

There was silence for a moment, as if Oleksiy was replaying the scene in his mind. "Thing is, it wouldn't be as much fun to watch from the farm. Nothin's fun on the farm. Even lyin' here hungry in a hayloft is better than being there with those cows."

Beneath them, they could hear the steady chewing of the animals. A rumble erupted from Janey's stomach. She shifted in the hay. "So, how old are you?"

"Twelve. And not much to show for it. Uncle Bill would only let me go to school when there wasn't much work on the farm. And just this mornin' he said I was too big to go back to school after Christmas. He says I don't need any-more schoolin'."

Janey could hear the bitterness in his voice. "You might be able to go to school when you get to the city. What do you want to be?"

"I don't know yet. All I know is that I want a job in the city an'...an'..." He paused, and switched gears. "Are your folks still alive?"

Janey wondered how much to tell him. "They are, but they're far away."

"Do you miss 'em?" The question came out as a whisper in the dark.

Janey thought about her mother in a distant country, trying to earn some money for them all, and her father, pacing the hospital hallways while her grandmother had her operation. "Yeah," she said. "A lot."

"You're lucky. At least they're still alive." The straw rus-tled beside Janey as Oleksiy turned.

"What happened to yours?"

"They died just after the war in the Old Country. They starved to death. There was no food. Neighbours found me in bed between them; I was just a baby."

"That must have been awful."

"I have no memory of it. Then someone remembered I had an uncle here in Canada, and brought me out here. I don't think he was happy to see me, though."

"Why not?"

"Well, I was another mouth to feed, and his wife...she just doesn't like me."

"So you ran away?"

"Yeah. This morning I snuck into the parlour and turned on the radio – I just wanted to hear if Wop May really was going to fly – and she caught me. She beat me with Uncle's belt and told me that a brat like me had no right to touch their radio." He paused a moment and swallowed loudly. "Then she said the only place for someone like me was in the cowshed."

Janey could taste the bitterness coming from Oleksiy.

"I don't only want to go back to school," he said, his voice suddenly fierce. "I want to grow up and have a good job and find a girl who'll love me and get us a cozy little house for our family." His voice petered away, then he laughed ruefully. "Listen to me goin' on about what I want, and here I hardly know you. But Uncle Bill just had girls until William was born, and he's only four. You can't talk to a four-year-old, or to girls." In the darkness, a small smile formed on Janey's lips.

Oleksiy shifted in the hay again, then said, "If I really had to say what I wanted, at least right now, it would be a job and a good winter coat and maybe a pair of mitts so's I can survive the winter. I want..." He sighed. "The trouble is, I want everything."

Janey lay silently beside him in the cold darkness. What was wrong with wanting everything? She wanted Granny to be fine, and to have her old life in Toronto, with her mum at home and her dad at work. Was that too much to ask?

Gradually, Oleksiy's breathing grew rhythmic and deep, and Janey abandoned her own wants and wishes for sleep.

WHEN THE BARN DOOR FLEW OPEN AGAIN, it was still dark. The same woman reappeared, struggling to shut the door against the wind that howled outside. Both Janey and Oleksiy peered over the edge of their loft, watching as she lit a lantern in the corner.

Again the woman went to work, filling pails with milk. She carried them both to the door, considered the sound of the wind, then put one down on the ground. She blew out the lantern, then left with the other one.

"Quick, before she gets back," Oleksiy urged, already halfway down the ladder. The cold, the clothes, and the darkness made Janey move slower than she wanted. By the time she reached the door, Oleksiy had already taken a good long gulp, drinking straight from the bucket. She took it from him, and felt the warmth of the milk spread through the tin and into her mittened hands. But before she could take a sip, the door swung open again, bashing the bucket from Janey's hands to the floor. Hot milk oozed through the layers of socks and running shoes, and Janey was so delighted with the warmth that she forgot to run. The woman reached out and grabbed her jacket.

"What are you doing here?" she said roughly, giving Janey such a hard shake that her head snapped back and her cap came off. Janey's ponytail tumbled out.

"You're a girl!" said two voices, one from the woman and one from the shadows beside her. The woman turned toward Oleksiy's voice.

"How many of you are in here?" she asked gruffly. Oleksiy moved into the light, looking at Janey with suspicion. "You let me blabber on last night about everything and you didn't even tell me you was a girl?" he growled.

The woman shook Janey again. "I said, how many of you are there?" Janey felt like she was being attacked on all sides.

"Just two. Just us. I'm Jamie...I mean, Janey Kane and this is Oleksiy Kanasewich."

The woman peered carefully at Janey. "I knew a Janey Kane once. Is she a relation?" She let go of Janey's coat and turned her face to the light.

"No," said Janey carefully. "There's just me, Janey."

"Odd," said the woman. "Same hair, same colour eyes. I would have sworn... Can you whistle?"

"Oh, for the love of... Girls don't whistle," said Oleksiy. He was staring belligerently at Janey, who'd just about had enough. She put her fingers in her mouth and let 'er rip. Again, both the woman and Oleksiy stood open-mouthed.

"But it's the same whistle, even," said the woman, softly.

Janey stared at her, trying to think things through. "When did you hear it before?" Janey asked.

"When I was a girl, and my family was camped in a tent by the river and these ladies thought..."

"Anna?" Now it was Janey's turn to be dumbfounded.

"Yes, I'm Anna. Anna Stanley. But back then I was Anna Hirczi." She looked at Janey thoughtfully, then said firmly, "You two must come with me. Inside. Where it's warm."

Janey could hardly move her milk-sodden feet. She stumbled along the path with Oleksiy so close behind her she could feel his breath on the back of her head.

Anna Stanley pushed open the door to the two-storey

farmhouse and they all crowded in. The room was large, lined with cupboards and equipped with a pump over a sink and a wood-burning cookstove. Janey's heart fell when she approached and realized it was stone cold.

"Come in to the winter kitchen. It's much warmer there," said Anna. She opened another door and led the way into a smaller, cosier kitchen. Anna poured them coffee from a pot simmering on the stove and Janey followed Oleksiy's example by adding three heaping spoons of sugar to the bitter brew.

While her feet thawed and her fingers grew warm, Janey tried to explain what she knew about why she was there. Oleksiy had made himself small in a corner and refused to comment, but Anna seemed to understand.

"Mama was so worried. She thought you'd disappeared forever into one of the old coal mine shafts. She sent Papa and Peter looking through all the abandoned tunnels, but they never found you."

"So does that mean that you were all right after the fire?" Janey looked fearfully at Anna, waiting for an answer.

"Well, we had to sleep on our neighbours' winter coats for a few nights, because our bedding was all wet," Anna said, laughing. "But the fire pushed Papa to leave the mines and really look for land. We were in our own house that Christmas."

"Anna, I have to know – did your doll survive?"

"My doll? You mean Henrietta?" Anna laughed softly.

"Come here," she said, grabbing Janey by the hand. She dragged her around the corner into the parlour. "Look," she said, lifting a cover off a doll's cradle. "This is where Elisabeth, our daughter, put her before going to visit her Oma over Christmas in the city."

"You have children?"

"Yes, two. Elisabeth and Thomas. And a husband, of course. Eric Stanley. He's in St. Albert this week, working on the telephones."

A crackle sputtered forth from a big wooden box in one corner.

"A radio!" said Oleksiy, showing enthusiasm for something for the first time since he'd found out about Janey. "Have you heard anything about the Mercy Flight?"

FOR THE NEXT THREE DAYS, while cold January winds whipped snow against the frozen landscape, the excited reports about Wop May and Vic Horner's daring flight into Canada's northern outposts gripped the little farmhouse, and indeed the whole province. Every delay, every emergency landing, every scramble for extra fuel was described in thrilled tones over the airwaves. When the radio announced that the Hudson's Bay Company man in Red River, the site of the original outbreak, had died before the medicine arrived, Janey blinked back tears and Oleksiy cleared his throat several times.

The pair had barely spoken to each other. Because the weather was too cold to leave, they had bunked down in the Stanley children's rooms, studiously avoiding any conversation. Oleksiy was wary around Janey, not sure what to think about her, while Janey was too wrapped up in her own worries. What was going on with Granny? she wondered. Was Dad coping, all by himself? When she got back to her own time, would they stay in Edmonton, or go back to Toronto? Sitting in the middle of that cold, white world was like being in her own eternal waiting room.

When the newsreader excitedly announced that the plane would return to Edmonton on the third afternoon, Oleksiy broke his silence with Janey. "I'm going back to that airport, even if I have to walk. From there I can get a ride with someone into town. You gonna stay here?"

Janey looked at the hazel eyes that were so similar to her own. "No, I'll come with you. I think I need to see the plane land."

THE CROWD WAS TEN TIMES as large as it had been when Wop May took off. Thousands of people were milling about, stamping their feet, clapping their hands, and scanning the overcast skies. The police officer who had stopped the children several days before seemed to have given up; the runway was clogged with onlookers.

Rumours went out that another plane had taken off to lead the heroes home, but bad weather had forced it back. It was already late when crowds heard the sputtering drone of an aircraft engine, and officials cleared a path on the runway.

In the press of bodies that surged forward, Janey and Oleksiy were carried to the front of the crowd. As the plane landed and taxied to a stop in front of them, loud cheers nearly deafened Janey. The pilots sat, seemingly transfixed, in the open cockpit.

Finally someone shouted, "They're frozen to the controls!" Several men rushed forward, pried the frozen fingers away, and lifted the pilots bodily from the plane.

"Take your goggles off, will ya, May, so we can get a good picture?" the reporters and photographers clamoured.

Someone reached over and pulled off the goggles, the helmet, the woollen muffler. Last came the silk scarf; Janey's silk scarf.

"Aahhh!"

Was it only Janey who heard Wop May's cry of pain? The crowd kept cheering while May fingered his mouth. Then his eyes fell on Janey. "You!" he said, working his way free and coming up to her. "You said this wouldn't freeze on my lips! Just look what it's done to me!"

Janey saw the blood oozing from the pilot's dry, frozen lips. Horrified, she turned and plunged into the crowd. How stupid of her, to think that a dumb little scarf was supposed to somehow save the life of her grandmother. She elbowed through the throng, frantically hoping that somehow the ground would swallow her up, as it had in the past.

No such luck. The hangar loomed ahead of her, and she ducked inside. Maybe she could find Daniel and he could... what?

Janey crumpled into a corner. She'd been a fool. What was she doing here? She'd have been more help sitting beside her dad in the waiting room, instead of stupidly thinking she could be of some help in something as important as this. Obviously she'd been wrong. And how was she supposed to get back, so she could sit with her dad and maybe hold her grandmother's hand when the operation was done? A wave of misery and homesickness washed over Janey and she began to sob.

"Janey?" The voice was anxious. She looked up and saw Oleksiy beside her, the bloody silk scarf dangling from his hand.

"Get that thing away from me," she snivelled, wiping away tears.

"But Janey, you should have heard him!" said Oleksiy, crouching down beside her.

"I did hear him. I practically heard the skin ripping from his lips when they took the stupid scarf off."

"Oh, he was just joking about that. You should have heard him later. He said the scarf is what probably saved the whole expedition."

Janey looked up. "Really?"

Oleksiy nodded. "He said that on the way up he'd forgotten he was wearing it and one of the ends came untucked and was flapping around behind him. He couldn't figure out what it was and turned around to look. That's when he noticed that the charcoal heater had caught fire. He said that without this scarf, he wouldn't have seen the fire until it was too late. They had to make an emergency landing to put out the fire, and then they travelled with the medicine inside their shirts, wrapped in this scarf."

"Really?" Had her scarf made the difference? Had *she* made a difference?

Oleksiy nodded again. Janey wished she had something

to blow her nose with, and briefly thought about the scarf. From deep in his overalls, Oleksiy pulled out a slightly dirty handkerchief and handed it, with the scarf, to her.

Janey took the handkerchief, blew hard, and then said, "Keep the scarf, Oleksiy. Look, I'm sorry if you thought I wasn't being honest with you, but I've got my own problems."

"Mr. May said something else, Janey. He said to tell you the Hudson's Bay man who died was named Logan, and is that any relation to the Logan girl you asked about."

Janey blinked. Was there any significance? Was *that* it? But if he died, then how...? She stood up, suddenly desperate to get back, to see if her grandmother was all right. "Thanks, Oleksiy. That helps a bit, but now all I want to do is go back to my own family and my own home."

She stood up. "The thing is, normally I seem to go through some kind of a hole, or a mining tunnel, or something, but in all this ice and snow, I'm not sure how..."

Two steps away from her was a trapdoor in the floor, the kind that might lead to a small underground storage space. She pulled open the covering and examined a ladder that descended into the darkness. Her body grew tingly and for the first time since she'd left the Stanley farm, she felt warm.

"Well, Oleksiy Kanasewich, I think it's time for me to go." He looked at her, puzzled. She could feel the heat coming out of the trapdoor, and was surprised Oleksiy hadn't noticed.

But the boy was looking at her from across the trapdoor. "Janey, I don't really understand you, but I'm sorry I was..." Janey cut him off by stepping toward him and handing him her jacket, mittens, and hat.

"I think," she said suddenly, looking more closely at the boy, "you'll be able to use these much more than me. Take care of them for me."

She pulled off the straps to the overalls and Oleksiy backed away. "No, don't worry, I've got other clothes underneath," she said, but paused. The heat from the trapdoor was rising. "Look, Oleksiy, I think you're going to do fine. I think you'll meet a lovely young woman in a red-and-white-striped dress and shoes that are a little too tight who will love you truly. And you will find her a beautiful house that she will cherish. And you will have a wonderful little family." She was rushing now, because the heat was making her dizzy. She leaned over, kissed the boy on the cheek, and stepped onto the first rung of the ladder.

"Remember me, Oleksiy." Then she disappeared.

CHAPTER NINE

THE LATE AUGUST SUN HAD WARMED GRANNY'S favourite bench in the ravine. It was a blue metal contraption shaped like a seated man and woman with a spaniel at their feet. Granny said it always reminded her of herself and Grampa.

Janey had convinced her dad to drive Granny to the closest path; then, with the help of Granny's cane, the two of them "hiked" the short gravel walk to the bench. It was the first time the old woman had been out since the operation.

Granny lowered herself gratefully onto the warmed metal, and patted the place beside it for her granddaughter. As Janey settled in, the locket clanged against the armrest.

"Tell me again, Granny, how your father died," said Janey, unsnapping the locket and studying the photo for the hundredth time.

"He had diphtheria," said Granny, idly watching a dog

and its master romp by. "It was lucky it didn't get me and Mother. But a famous flyer by the name of Wop May flew up with an antitoxin. Without it, we all would have died. They made a big to-do about it in the press in those days." Her eyes seemed focused on things other than the ravine for a moment, then turned to her granddaughter.

"But you don't want to hear me go on about the olden days, do you, kiddo?"

"I don't mind, Granny. Sometimes, when you talk, it all seems so real to me."

Granny chuckled. "I'd forgotten about your fascination with Fort Edmonton Park. Will you go there this weekend when your mum comes out?"

Janey shook her head. She'd been back one last time, and had watched the construction workers pour concrete to create the floor of the hangar. She knew her adventures at the park were over.

Besides, Janey had chosen a new path for adventures. After the long weekend, she was starting junior high in Edmonton. The twins had promised to save her a place at the cafeteria table at lunch. And she and Nicky were thinking about trying out for the basketball team.

"I think I just want our family to hang out together," said Janey finally. "There's so little time before school starts." She sighed.

"Are you worried about fitting in at school, kiddo?"

Janey didn't look at her grandmother, but finally said, "I'm worried about that, and about you, and about Mummy working so far away and Daddy with no job..."

She paused to admire the first yellow leaves on the ground beside her. They reminded Janey of her sunflowers, growing tall and strong in Granny's garden.

The old woman smiled and reached for her granddaughter's hand. "Kiddo, I think things will work out just fine." She gave the hand a squeeze. "Just fine."

AUTHOR'S NOTES

THIS IS A WORK OF HISTORICAL FICTION. While many of the characters are creations, others, such as John Rowand, Wop May, Emily Murphy, Lovisa McDougall and Margaret Henderson were real people. I have tried to show them in the context of their times, whether as the impatient chief factor pounding on the floorboards overhead (Rowand), a scared and lonely young mother newly arrived in the wilderness (McDougall), or a busy farm woman and midwife with no time to listen to the ditherings of a young girl (Hen-derson).

Incidents such as the 1929 Mercy Flight, temperance marches, vigilante groups, tent cities, and the prejudice against non-English-speaking immigrants were real. Wop May was given a white silk scarf before taking off to Fort Vermillion, though his son, Denny May, says there's no record of how he got it. May and Horner were forced to land because the brazier caught fire.

Some historical events formed the basis of fictional char-acters. The ghost story about King and his daughter (Louisa's mother) is related in the 1803 diary of the North West Company director at the time, but Louisa and her family are fictional. The unfortunate Mr. George did have his house pulled over the North Saskatchewan cliffs, but there is no evidence he had a son called Lucas. A Hudson's Bay Com-pany manager in Red River did die of diphtheria, but there is no indication he had a daughter called Amanda. The characters of Martin, Anna, and Oleksiy are my own inventions, as are those in the modern-day portions of the book.

ACKNOWLEDGEMENTS

WITHOUT THE KIND AND HELPFUL STAFF at Fort Edmonton Park, especially Tim Marriott, this book would not have been written. I would like to thank Denny May, who graciously took the time to answer questions about his father's adventures, while Ted Allcock walked this city girl through the steps of field dressing a deer. Marjorie Memnook from the University of Alberta explained the origins of First Nations names and helped me christen Janey's rescuer in Chapter Two. The librarians at the Edmonton Public Library are an under-acknowledged treasure. I am also grateful to Barbara Sapergia's critical eye and gentle hand; they make her a wonderful editor. Any errors of fact are mine.

I relied on the work of many writers and researchers, including Alex Mair's *Gateway City,* Tony Cashman's *The Edmonton Story,* Elizabeth M. McCrum's *Letters of Lovisa McDougall 1878-1887,* and Victoria MacLean's lovely descriptions of homesteading on the Prairies, in *Alberta in the 20th Century,* volume 2.

It was a joy for me to read my work-in-progress to the kids in Frau Karner's 2002–2003 class at Forest Heights School; their enthusiastic support and suggestions were invaluable.

Finally, to Emma, Sarah, and Gordon, my love and thanks – you are my home, anywhere in the world.

ABOUT THE AUTHOR

RITA FEUTL HAS BEEN A WRITER since she was seven, when she finally learned enough English to string sentences together. After that, she could barely take her nose out of books while she was growing up in Toronto. She has a BA from the University of Toronto, an MA from the University of Western Ontario and a post-graduate diploma in Teaching English as a Second Language from the University of Alberta.

When she's not teaching English in Istanbul, climbing the Great Wall of China, or sharing news-gathering skills with reporters in Tanzania, Rita is a writer and journalist. Her work has appeared in publications across the country, including *The Globe and Mail, The Toronto Star,* and the *Edmonton Journal.* She lives in Edmonton with her husband and two daughters.